I0757956

TALES FROM THE JAIL

Fictional Composite Novel
Synopsis

MARIE-GHISLAINE MERA

ISBN 978-1-956696-44-8 (paperback)
ISBN 978-1-956696-45-5 (digital)

Copyright © 2021 by Marie-Ghislaine Mera

All rights reserved. No part of this publication may be reproduced, distributed, or transmitted in any form or by any means, including photocopying, recording, or other electronic or mechanical methods without the prior written permission of the publisher. For permission requests, solicit the publisher via the address below.

Rushmore Press LLC
1 800 460 9188
www.rushmorepress.com

Printed in the United States of America

CHAPTER 1

The storytellers in this novel are prisoners and their visitors. They tell stories of their lives, their past, and what they have heard or told. In jail, they question their faith and challenge some deeply rooted religious doctrines.

They tell about what leads to their incarceration. Some reconnect with their spirituality and question their conscience. In jail, they tell stories to pass the time and create a friendly atmosphere.

Errol Francis relates his chilling experience in his fictional story of when Lucifer visited his native town of San Marco to question his worshipers, know why they worship him, confront his accusers, learn why they make him responsible for their sins, and intimidate a non-believer who does not believe in his existence at all. Simon is a single man who took a homeless cat home to soon realize that the kitten embodies the spirit of his dead mother and became a poltergeist to haunt him.

Kate, who visited her sister Emile in jail, recounts the mysterious tale of a cow, jumping off the slaughtering table screaming, "God, have mercy on me!" causing a riot in a small town. The cow killed the vendor who was waiting for its meat in the marketplace.

Vietnam war veteran, Walt, narrates his favorite fictional story about slavery in Saint Domingue. It is about twin brothers, Hector and Homer, who arrived in Saint Domingue as slaves. Hector met an untimely death. Homer avenged his brother then foiled the French settlers when he introduced them to an addictive cocktail drink.

Vincent Manchester is a racist who sent a young black man to prison for a crime he did not commit. Sara Manchester, coerced by her father, accused his black friend of sexual assault. Vincent Manchester was never told the truth about his mulatto half-siblings in Jamaica. Martha Manchester is a racist who went to the extreme to keep her white children apart from their mulatto half-brothers.

Eli is a seventy-five-year-old man who describes a miracle that happened to a girl called Sadia who was rejected by society because of her disfigurement. After a strange rainfall in the city of Capernaum USA, Sadia was cured because Jesus Christ came to visit Capernaum.

Ilda, a woman prisoner, remembers how Fanny was heartbroken after seeing her presumably dead husband alive in an Indian village in Sonora, Mexico. The reality set in for Fanny. Kaleb is alive and he has a young Indian wife and a baby girl.

Brooklyn County Jail

Errol Francis is arrested on a DUI charge. In jail, he met a few others with DUI charges and other felonies. At some point, the prisoners were bored, and one of them said, "Can anyone tell a joke or a story? I want to take my mind off my problems." "Yes." Someone agreed and added, "Anybody has a guitar or something to entertain us? It is getting really boring here." Errol Francis replied, "I can tell a story, a joke. I can even sing." One voice said, "But you are drunk. What kind of story can you possibly tell?"

Errol began, "Once upon a time." A man said, "Hey! Hey! I don't want to hear any three little pigs, Goldilocks, or Cinderella. I want to hear stories for real men, adult stories. I like mystery, thriller, magic, and sex, bro." Errol replied, "I would like a drink to help me remember better." They all laughed, and Jose said to Errol, "Are you out of your fricking mind, man? You are in jail and you are asking for booze. Unbelievable!"

John said, "And since when booze can improve memory?" One voice said, "Alright! Storyteller, start telling your story. It better be a good one or we will say boo!" Errol begged, "No, no, do not do that.

Just pretend to fall asleep(snore) if you want to. I will feel embarrassed if you boo me." Everybody said, "Okay."

Errol started, "In the summer of 1990, a Saturday if I remember correctly, an entity arrived in San Marco, my hometown in Texas near the Mexican border. The entity was taller than any human being I have ever seen. His face was of a whitish complexion with a flat affect. His hair was long and jet black, his eyes were fiery red, his teeth were yellowish, his ears were elongated and stick out, and his voice was like thunder. His breath was hot, enough to make anyone who encounters him sweat." Someone said, "Excuse me. May I make a comment? Not a serious one, though. You said his face was white as in white people, his hair black as in black folks, his teeth yellow as in Asian, his eyes red as in native American, his ears long and pointy as in alien. So, the devil is made of all the races and all the races have a little devil in them, and moreover, there is a little bit of alien in all of us." The prisoner laughed at his own joke. One man whispered to another, "Is this dude okay?" The other whispered back, "He sounds a little crazy, but he has a point. In popular belief, anything that is negative, obscure, no good, is always black. For instance, the devil is often represented as black. Ham, the son of Noah, in the bible was black. There was a terrible plague in circa 1300 in Europe. It was called the black death. You see what I mean." The other man shook his head and said, "You have a point, man."

And Errol continued to relate, "As the entity stopped at the police station to check-in, the police officer just looked at him and fainted. The other officers were petrified. Their tongue became heavy and their legs gave out. One tried to ask him for his identity; his speech became slurred and he was trembling like a leaf, stuttering. 'What is the purpose of your visit, sir?' He replied in the loudest voice ever with a question, 'What is your purpose on planet earth, you?' Then he went through; suddenly, he turned into a ball of fire moving in the air. The level of anxiety was high. Everyone was mystified by such a mysterious event. The police got involved but alas, the entity was elusive. The police were powerless because he could turn from a ball of fire into a cloud, and then into a physical being again. The news spread fast. Everybody in town was told to remain at home fearing that the entity would attack."

Jose said, "That's really spooky, man. Who was he, anyway, an alien?"

Errol replied calmly, "No, his name was Bel Za Lux (Lux for Lucifer)."

John said, "Oh! I see, the bible has Beelzebub or Satan who is really Lucifer (angel of light), the most beautiful of all angels. He rebelled against the creator. Consequently, he was demoted, sent to earth, wandering in the universe, and causing troubles to mankind. So, the devil really visited your town, but why?"

Errol answered, "Because there was a sanctuary called the church of Lucifer. Most of the rich and educated people in town worshiped the devil. They did not want to worship God. They chose to adopt the devil, causing a clash between them and the Christians continuously. I am sorry. I am kind of hungry now. Are they going to give us a snack or something to munch on?"

A prisoner replied, "Hey, bro, you are not home. There is no late snack unless you are a diabetic. So, keep talking. I am interested in your story."

Errol continued, "All reporters in town were eager to have a glance at him. The next day, he visited the church of Lucifer. The worshipers were in their satanic costumes. Some were naked, as usual, ready to worship. They began their service by saying 'Hail, Satan!' But they were shocked when an extra loud and echoing voice hailed back to them. 'Hail evil, you!' Most of them fell unconscious. The leader, in dismay, kept looking around to see where the voice was coming from. Finally, in his quivering voice, he asked, 'Who are you? We are not afraid of you.' Lucifer laughed loudly, so loud that the building oscillated. All worshipers were lying flat on their stomach speechless, trying to reach each other's hand to hold on to. Some were murmuring, 'Let me get out of here. I don't come here to die. Michael should have a prayer to send him away.'

The leader, all shook up, continued asking, 'What do you want from us? Are you an alien?'

The entity replied, 'Why do you worship me, really? Did I ever ask anyone to worship me? Did I create you? Did I give you commandments to follow? Did I send any prophets to talk to you? Did I send a prophet like Moses to talk to you and a redeemer named

Jesus? I never promised you immortality. Have you learned somewhere that I am eternal, omnipotent, omniscient, omnipresent, good, just, and able of loving? Did I ever do anything good for anybody? Your creator Elohim does all the good, and I am responsible to do evil only. So, why do you have a beautiful temple erected in my name? Because you are inherently evil. The end is near, and the wall is closing in. Jesus will come back to defeat me because of you. I do not want to be defeated nor destroyed. I have plans and you are messing up things for me.' The leader uttered, 'What kind of plans, if I may ask?' Satan replied, 'To regain my rightful place in heaven, next to Elohim the ruler of the universe, as it was in the beginning.' The leader expressed loudly, 'You are nothing.' While he was chatting with Satan, the members got out of the premises one by one quietly. He looked around and see nobody. The temple was emptied.

The dialogue between the two continued. Satan told him, 'You have seventy-two hours to destroy this building or dedicate it to something else. If you do not, there will be serious consequences.' The leader replied defiantly, 'Such as?' Satan declared, 'All firstborns will die. Your water will turn into urine, so will the nursing mother's milk. Your foods, your crops will rot, your money will disappear, your pets will attack you, and this structure you call temple will burn down to ashes. You have seventy- two hours to comply.'

The next day, the leader of the church called his mother and asked, 'Mom, I have an important question to ask you.' 'What is it, son?' Michael asked, 'Am I your firstborn?' The mom replied, 'What kind of question is that? Of course, you are my first.' Michael said, 'How about the pregnancy before me?' The mother replied, 'I had a miscarriage. How could it be first? And what is this question really about? What's going on?' Michael said, 'Nothing, nothing, I just asked. Thank you, mom.' He was very troubled because his wife and daughter are first-born."

One man made a comment, "What a selfish son of a bitch! He was thinking only about himself. 'Am I first, mom?'" The auditors burst out laughing regarding Michael who realized that his wife and his daughters are also firstborns.

"Then, he wanted to negotiate with the entity. In the meantime, the Christians were rejoicing to hear that the devil worshipers were running away from the devil because they were terrified by his overwhelming presence. Some of them tried to skip town. They got into fatal accidents. An elder of the congregation advised Michael to have a press conference, letting the media and the community know about the entity and his demands and ultimatum. The news was out, resulting in a riot. Believers and non-believers were out to destroy the church of the devil. Some devil worshipers were quick to deny their faith, claiming that they never really believed in the devil. They go to church by curiosity and for financial support. The rich worshipers would financially support anybody who accepts to convert to satanism."

Errol said, "A lot happened during these seventy-two hours. Satan went to visit an atheist."

Tyrone, one of the listeners, said, "He went to visit an atheist, why?" Jose replied, "Because atheists don't believe in anything but in their knowledge." "I am an atheist. I don't believe in anything," declared Tyrone. And Jose replied, "Except in booze and drug. You are a bum, man. God doesn't want you. Satan doesn't need you either."

Omar, another inmate, said, "I am Muslim. I believe in Allah and I hate atheists." Errol said, "Okay, let me continue. Do you want me to stop?" Everybody said, "No, No! What did he say to the atheist?"

"Karl Mendelson was a physicist in town and a professor at San Marco University. One evening, he heard that big voice saying to him. 'I do not exist for you, right?' Karl looked around him and didn't see anybody, so he did not answer. The voice said again, 'You don't acknowledge my existence, right?' Finally, Karl answered by asking, 'Who the hell are you?' 'I am Lucifer,' he replied. Karl was disconcerted by the response. He did not know what to make of it or what to say. 'Lucifer.' He was baffled, then he confided to his wife that he heard a voice. The wife told him that his imagination was running wild. Due to the story of the devil and all going around now, the wife ignored him.

The devil asked him again, 'Do you believe that the devil exists?' Karl, although frightened, replied, 'Hell, no! In the name of Jesus, go away!' Satan laughed loudly and Karl's wife, his children, and the servant started laughing also for no apparent reason. Not knowing what they were laughing about, the wife became frenzied, the children were jumping around with tears in their eyes, the dogs started barking for no reason, the cats meowed and were fighting each other, his piano started playing by itself, and Karl became profoundly confused. He got his coat on to get out, then the voice said, 'I am going to show you that Satan exists because he was created.' Karl, still stubborn, replied, 'Go ahead, show me.' Satan said, 'Before you reach that luxury car, it will explode on your face." At this point, Karl hesitated to go to his car. In a split second, there was a big boom! The car exploded."

Jose laughed and said, "I don't get it. Karl is an atheist, and he was calling on Jesus' name to chase the devil. I know atheists are bluffing. A lot of them call themselves atheists because they are educated, but, when facing danger or great fear, they call on to God."

The auditors asked, "What happened to the rest of his family?" Errol replied, "The wife was confused for seventy-two hours. The children were traumatized by the explosion and were eventually treated by psychologists." "Where did Lucifer go next?" someone asked.

"He paid a visit to a pastor who talked too much about him, making him responsible for all Christians' sins. Thus, it was nighttime. The pastor and his wife were about to go pray when suddenly, the pastor heard a loud voice and felt extremely hot and aware of an immense presence in the room. He was sweating. His wife asked, 'What is it? You are sweating. You look pale. Should I call the doctor?' 'No, no that is not necessary,' he uttered and fell on his knees to pray. And a voice said to him, 'You believe in me too much, you. You called me a liar. Am I the only liar there is, Pastor? You have a child with another woman. Should I tell your wife for you, or will you tell the truth and stop lying to all and repeatedly stating "Satan is a liar"? That is your favorite phrase every Sunday—repeating that to everybody—Satan is a liar. Remember that line. Every Sunday you make your congregation, say that you are also a liar. Let me advise you. Stop talking about me. I am bad, it is true, but you, mankind, is no angel. You are genetically evil. Do not put all the blames on me. Elohim chose to give you all kinds of emotions, allowing you to have all kinds of feelings that you cannot control. They say that I am the one responsible for all evil in the world. It sounds true, but in fact, power, sex, and money are the roots of all evil in the world, and they are all at man's fingertips. I did not create them, did I? I am no creator. I can only destroy, not create.' The pastor, in fear, agreed with him and said, 'Yes, yes, Satan, I lied.' He then bent down to ask God for forgiveness and confessed to his wife about his ongoing infidelity and about the child he conceived with a younger woman in the church. The wife forgave him, but his congregation put him on probation.

Then, Satan went to talk to a preacher who once declared in a sermon that it was the devil who put Christ on the cross.

Samuel Gordon, a well-known preacher, was getting ready to record a sermon for his ministry when he heard a voice. He was not surprised since the story of Satan in town was a hot topic. Lucifer said to him, 'You claimed that I put Jesus on the cross. You do not even know Jesus. Do you honestly believe that I, Lucifer, put him on the cross, or do you mean that your wrongdoings forced him to come down on planet earth to save you from eternal destruction? You are not dignified to teach anyone if you can make such a statement. By saying that, you make Jesus, someone like you, a powerless, sinful human being. Nobody placed Jesus on the cross. He chose to do so. It was not Judas, not Pilate, not Caiaphas, not the Romans. He wanted to be immolated on the cross to save humanity. He used those who were already doomed, no good, deplorable souls to accomplish his mission. Jesus was humble. He came to earth as a poor man. I would not do that. He sat on a donkey to enter Jerusalem. I would not do that either because I am immensely proud and conceited. I would come to this world as the son of a rich earthly king, enter Jerusalem on a high white horse, escorted by soldiers or on a golden chariot, and followed by an army of hell angels. Jesus exchanged his crown for a cross to save you from annihilation. Do you really deserve all that? I do not think so. You are just like the crowd who followed him to Golgotha, a riot of beggars, scaredy-cats who would not take the sword or not even a rock, to defend their Lord. They kept back, watching the Romans crucify their king. How coward were they!'

The preacher said to him, 'According to the apostles, you tempted Jesus, remember, after his fasting in the Judean desert.'

Satan screamed, 'Oh! Oh! That is a lie! I cannot even get close to Jesus. How could I tempt him? With what? I have nothing. Once again, you do not understand him at all. He went alone into the Judean desert, an awful place, crowded with all kinds of terrible crawling creatures: snakes, vipers, scorpions, and all. He went alone to test his divinity. He remained forty days and forty nights without food and any drink. As a divinity, he could do it. But when he took on his human nature, he was hungry—so, so hungry that he hallucinated; he saw me; he heard me; he saw fresh bread; he heard voices; he saw a cliff like any normal human would if he survived the fast, which is very unlikely. His disciples pinned that on me. If I did take him to the Judean Desert, for what purpose? I got too many credits. For the record, it was not me. As a human being, Jesus was hungry, damn it! It was not me doing anything to him. Oh! That is what his apostles, those cowards, wrote about me. I never knew that until recently. Hey, listen to me carefully, preacher. I want you to retract that statement about me putting Jesus on the cross. You must retract it within seventy-two hours.' The preacher defiantly asked, 'If I don't . . . because I am not afraid of you in the name of Jesus.' Satan replied, 'You like to make statements, so, you will lose your speech. How about that? Remember, you have seventy-two hours.'

The preacher knew that Satan is able of evil. He went on TV and tell that he was greatly mistaken when he said Satan put Jesus on the cross. He was surprised by the viewer's response. They did not agree with him either for making such a statement. His viewers think he speaks too much of Satan. He does not know how to preach at all. The preacher was disappointed by his followers' comments and attitude."

Jose asked, "What about Michael, the leader, what did he do?" Errol responded, "Before seventy-two hours, the building was turned into an orphanage and a shelter. People rushed to bring everything needed for the shelter and the orphanage. His wife Marla converted to Christianity with her daughter Patty. Michael was too proud to convert to any faith, so soon." Tyrone said, "There is no God." An older man called Eli replied furiously, "How dare you? You dare to say there is no God in front of me. You are an atheist. I do not care for you but stating loudly there is no God is disrespectful. If you repeat that again, I will beat the shit out of you. Who the hell are you to say there is no God? In seventy-two hours, I will beat the shit out of you if you repeat that nonsense again. You understand?"

Tyrone stated ironically, "Yes, pop, I got you. But you are kind of frail to beat the shit out of me."

It was funny. Everybody laughed. They thought Eli was sleeping. Instead, he was listening to the story quietly.

John asked, "Who will be the next to be visited by Satan?" Errol answered, "The Catholic priest, but I am tired now and it is getting late; I'll continue tomorrow."

The next day, John asked Eli, "Why are you locked up?" "For public exposure. I was taking a leak in a park. That is all. I have nothing much to expose. The police are crazy," he stated. Errol got back and he asked, "Do you still want to hear the story?" "Yes," everybody said. Omar asked, "Before you continue, tell us what happened to Karl, the atheist." Errol replied, "He became mentally disturbed. He was walking around in his neighborhood, disheveled, repeating incessantly 'Satan does exist, Satan does exist, yes, he does, yes, he does.'" John asked, "Who was next in Satan's list to visit?" Errol said, "The catholic priest." The audience commented, saying, "Wow! Lucifer was after the clergymen."

"Satan went to the rectory to visit Father William, an exorcist who was just about to go see a church member supposedly possessed by the devil. So, he was getting ready to exorcise an evil spirit. He had his cross, a small container of holy water, his exorcism book, and the bible in his hand. Satan inquired, 'Why do you need a cross and holy water to cast out the devil?' Father William could not answer. Satan continued, 'A cross is a manmade artifact, and it's supposed to scare me away. Holy water, what makes the water holy, Father? After today, you will never use a cross again.' Father William attempted to reach the cross. His upper limbs became numb. So, he tried to say 'In the name of Jesus' but his speech was slurred, so he said it in his heart. Surprisingly, Satan left him alone."

Tyler said, "You see that the name of Jesus only sent him away. What is the business with the cross? Why does a cross mean so much to people? On a stupid cross, Jesus died, and yet, instead of hating the cross, they venerate it. The cross is supposed to be a painful reminder to Christians. That is why I stay away from religion. They do not know a shit of what they are doing." Jose asked, "Who will be next?" Errol said, "A shaman/voodoo/ sorcerer." Tyler said, "You don't say San Marco has voodoo?" Errol replied, "Of course, it is a multicultural town. There are all kinds of religions: Santeria, Voodoo, etc. Satan went to visit a magician in town named Pablo who, unlike everybody else, was expecting him. He was elated to meet Satan who looked around his peristyle and saw all kinds of macabre decorations and ornaments. 'What is this all about?' Satan asked. The magician proudly replied, 'All is for you, majesty. I have been waiting for this moment. My name is Pablo. I have been worshipping you since childhood. My whole family adores you. I understand you, but I don't understand God at all. Now that I meet you, it's my chance to request all that I want. Grant me power, power to turn any metal into gold, any rock into precious gems. Grant me the power to fly, to turn an enemy into any animal I wish, to make rain fall upon my wish, and even to manipulate the sun. And for that, me and my household will glorify your name forever, majesty.' Satan said, 'You are overly ambitious. Very well. In half-hour, all your dreams and desires will be fulfilled. Goodbye, Pablo.' Pablo bowed grandiosely (all the way down) to him."

John said, "I can't wait to see what will happen in a half-hour. Satan is lying to him." Everybody said, "Yes, he is lying to him because Pablo is bad, greedy. He only begged, begged, and begged. He is a bad seed on earth."

CHAPTER 2

Errol related, "Half an hour later, Pablo felt that he could not stay inside his house. He had the urge to go out in the field. Suddenly, he wanted to eat grass. His genitals were enlarging. He was feeling strong like a horse."

"Raaaaaaah!" (Laughter) The inmates were laughing loudly and hysterically, uttering, "Strong as a horse, his penis and testicles were getting out of proportion." "Hahaha. He will turn into a horse, I bet you," someone declared.

Errol said, "Let me finish. Pablo walked to his backyard, then felt extremely sleepy. He laid down on the grass. He fell asleep. When he woke up, he was turned into a big brown horse. He got up and went to the house trying to get in, but he could not. He acted like a horse would. He brayed constantly, hoping someone would understand him. At the end of the day, when Pablo did not come home, his wife Elena was concerned. Then, she noticed a horse on her lawn eating the grass. She got mad and called the city to come to pick it up since nobody seems to know the owner. There was no stamp on the horse. The city took the horse. A couple of days later, it was sold to the highest bidder in an auction. In the meantime, Elena made a police report for her missing husband. The horse was already sold to the highest bidder who was Pablo's worst rival, Salvatore Delgado, the very person he wanted to turn into an animal.

He was taken to the barn. There, Pablo (as a horse) started praying to God. 'Please, God, forgive me for choosing the devil over you. Please do not let me be a horse forever. Send an angel to deliver me. You delivered Jonah from the belly of a whale. Please deliver me from evil. I was blind, now I see.'"

Jose and others started singing amazing grace, while some were laughing. Errol continued, "Elena went to see Salvatore (her ex-husband, Pablo's mortal enemy) to ask him if he did something to Pablo. Salvatore laughed saying ironically, 'What can I possibly do to a magician like Pablo? It is like asking me what I did to the devil. Pablo is a great magician. He disappeared and will eventually reappear.'

Elena upset, replied, 'What do you mean by eventually? Do you know something I don't?' Salvatore replied, 'Whenever he has a chance to return, he will return. If he wants to return, that's what I meant. By the way, later, would you do me the honor to take a horseback ride with me? So, I can try my new wandering horse.' Elena responded harshly, 'Are you out of your mind? My husband is missing, and you want me to take a horseback ride with you? How insensitive of you!' Salvatore smiled and spoke, 'You will change your mind. Nobody will see us. We will go to the country to have a wonderful time as usual.' 'Don't count on it,' exclaimed Elena.

Two days later, Salvatore picked Elena up and took her to the barn. They got on the horse. They were riding Pablo as a horse. After the ride, Salvatore tied the horse that he named Bacchus to a tree. Elena laid a blanket on the green lawn to have a picnic. When the picnic was over, they got back on the horse who got wild, jumped high, and kicked them off his back to the ground. Both were seriously injured. Pablo said to himself, 'Elena is still cheating on me. I should kill them both.'

Then, a Christian father came out in the street with his bible in his hand to exhort Satan. He started by screaming, 'You, anathema!' His ten-year-old son, Philip, came out and said, 'No, dad. He is going to come after you. Don't scream. Don't talk too much.' He claimed proudly, 'I can face him. I am not afraid of him.'

Philip reminded his father of what Jesus said, 'Do not resist the devil, dad, remember. You simply must speak firmly with authority, like this, "The Lord is my shepherd; I shall not want. When I walk through the streets of my hometown, I shall fear no evil, no devil, no

Satan.'" And he continued praying, reciting the psalm 91. He ended his prayer by saying 'in the name of Jesus I pray, and I order you, Lucifer, to move on. Get out of town now.'

The words of the ten-year-old boy subdued him. Before getting out of town, Lucifer addressed the residents of San Marco for the last time, 'At noon on Saturday, I will be leaving. There will be a strong wind. All doors should be closed. No peeking through the keyhole. My physical self will be magisterial, impressive, marvelous, but nobody should see that grandiosity. Just like you can't see Elohim and live, you can't see me either and live.' His speech was intended simply to tempt people to look at him leaving.

Some teenagers, despite their parents' recommendations not to look, found a way to watch him leaving. They saw him and some of them momentarily passed out. They all had bloodshot in their eyes for days."

"What's happened to Pablo?" asked another listener. Errol replied, "At the barn where he was kept, he turned back into a human and went home. He never told his wife what happened to him. His life had changed once a magician became a believer. After Satan left, everybody got back to normal. All the crosses in the church were gone for good. Karl Mendelson became a believer. Michael, the leader of the Satan church, left town. Nobody knew what happened to him. His wife and daughter remained in town as fervent Christians.

The following week, the residents of San Marco took over the streets in prayer. Christians of all faiths got together for a big revival, and it was beautiful and emotional to see how they all got together as a community and as Christians in the face of adversity."

Tyler said, "How odd! It takes the devil to unite believers. What a story, man!" John said, "I have a question, Errol. Why did the pastor's wife forgive him so easily knowing how women can be a tyrant when it comes to infidelity? They can make your life a living hell. The nagging would go on and on." Errol didn't have to answer that; somebody else responded, "The devil was there; she was frightened. Besides, she probably had her own secrets. So, she had to play cool in a moment like that, man. She will get him later."

Errol said, "Eli, what do you think of what Satan said about the apostles being cowards?" Eli replied, "Before resurrection, they were cowards because they didn't fully understand Jesus. Peter denied him, the others went on hiding, Judas betrayed him, and the crowd who was after him for miracles turned against him and forsake him. After the resurrection, all changed. I understand Satan's points, but I stick to the bible because it's the first and foremost authority on the history of the creation. Until there is something more accurate, the bible prevails." "Well. I agree with you," said Errol.

"In the aftermath, the incident became a big joke. You could hear people say, 'I give you seventy-two hours to pay me back, or, if you don't come back in seventy-two hours, I will . . .' Salvatore was desperately looking for his wandering horse. A neighbor told him that he saw Pablo coming out of his barn earlier. He ignored the information. He made a police report."

Jose put down his guitar and said, "I have a story to tell, guys." "Okay. We are listening."

"There was a man named Simon. He was a bachelor who lived with his female cat named Ellie who was once a street cat. One night, Simon parked his old Chevy Impala car and was walking home from work around one o'clock in the morning. Then, he noticed that a cat was following him. When he got home, the cat wanted to get in. He chased him away, even though he felt sorry for the feline. He did not want to invite him in. For three days, the cat followed him home. He concluded that the cat is a street cat. So, he took it in. He had her spayed, vaccinated, did all that need to be done for a cat. It was a female cat, so he called her Ellie who became his indispensable companion.

From a sheriff sale, he purchased a house and turned it into a beautiful home, for him and Ellie. Ellie had her own room. They were both happy until some strange events were taking place in the house. Simon said to himself, 'Did I buy a haunted house?' The cat was acting strangely the very first day. She went from room to room meowing and got into Simon's messy bedroom meowing like she wanted to say something. Simon was concerned. He tried to understand why Ellie always complained. He left his bedroom a mess: bed not made, his clothes in disarray on the floor, his closet open, and his room always untidy. He does not mind a messy room. Since the arrival of the cat, he came home every day finding to his great surprise, his bed made, his clothes nicely put away, his bathroom straightened up, and his trash picked up. He was highly apprehended. He was getting frightened of living in his own house.

Because all doors were locked, he had nobody to come to clean for him. His mom died long ago. He checked all entrances in his house, no breaking anywhere. He told his friends about his experience. They told him that the house is definitely haunted."

Tyler said, "It sounds mysterious, but it's not typical of a haunted house. Usually, you would hear a noise; you would see shadows. I have never heard of such a case."

Jose continued, "Simon called a priest to exorcise the house. Nothing changed. At least, once a week, there was a supernatural occurrence. He came home. The whole house smelled like a perfume his mother used to love and used all the time till her death. That smell puzzled him and lingered in his mind. 'Why do I smell my mother's perfume all the time?'

So, he spoke to a minister who came with some members of his congregation to pray for him and exhorted the supposed spirit that inhabited the house.

For a few months, everything went well. There were no supernatural activities. Simon who planned to put the house for sale changed his mind. For Thanksgiving, he went away to visit his family members in Boston. He left the cat with plenty of food and water. When he returned, he found his front door lock broke. He was scared to get in. He did not have his gun with him. So, he proceeded to enter cautiously just in case the intruder was still in. Nothing could have prepared him for what he witnessed in his living room—a dead man covered with blood, his face all scratched. Next to him were Simon's laptop, his TV, his brand-new guitar, and his safe where he kept his gun and some cash. He was in shock. He ran upstairs. In the hallway was another man lying down in blood, dead. Simon was distraught. He did not know what to do. He called a friend who advised him to call the police right away.

The police came. The victims were taken away. The two burglars were already on the police list to be captured. However, the mystery remained—who attacked them? Simon spent hours, days, and months of interrogation. The police could not understand the supernatural aspect of the case. They laughed at Simon when he told them about his room being cleaned and his clothes nicely put away for him. However, when he mentioned the smell of his mother's perfume, a senior officer took note and said, 'Your mother's spirit is visiting you.' And he added, 'Who else lives here with you?' 'Ellie, my cat.' The officer swiftly remembers the scratches on the men's faces and all over the body. Then, he asked, 'How big is your cat?' Simon replied, 'Is that relevant to the case?' The police said, 'I want to see the cat. I want her prints.' Simon went to get Ellie; she was nowhere to be found. Nobody let her out. Ellie disappeared for days and then reappeared in her room, sitting on the windowsill. Simon was baffled and became superstitious, asking himself, 'Could the cat be the one who attacked the . . .? No, what a crazy idea. It is a small cat. What am I thinking? On the other hand, why did the cat disappear, then reappear? I did not let it out. I did not let it in. Something about Ellie is not right. Could my Ellie be a "she-devil," a mysterious cat?'

Simon was asked by the police not to leave town until they figure out who was the third intruder who killed the two burglars. The story was on TV and in newspapers. Families and friends came by to bring support to Simon. His sister encouraged him to sell the house. Mark, his neighbor, told him that he had heard a lot of noises coming from his house while he was away. He thought Simon was home or the screaming was from the television since he likes to keep his television loud."

Tyrone interrupted to ask, "But, why would Simon think that the cat has something to do with the attack? A normal cat, regardless of his size, can't beat two men to death. That's irrational."

Jose continued, "Anyway, when his sister Denise came to see him, he told her that once the investigation is over, he is going to Louisiana to seek the advice of a shaman. He would like her to stay in the house for him while he will be gone. Denise declared, 'I am sorry. I will not stay in a house that is haunted. I can take the cat home if you want. Besides, what are you going to see a shaman for? Are you out of your mind? Since when men are interested in seers? I am surprised. You, going away to seek a seer? Just liquidate the house. What do you think a seer is going to do? Most of them lie. Let me tell you what happened to a friend of mine. Her husband consulted a shaman who promised super protection at the cost of $500. He assured him that nothing will ever happen to him and his family and he will prosper. When her husband died, she opened the envelope that contained the so-called super-protection which has been posted on the front door for years. When she opened it, she saw a doll pillow. She cut it. Do you know what was inside that cost five hundred bucks? The psalm 91 handwritten in red ink.'"

John started laughing, saying, "When I get out of here, I am going to sell psalms. That's a good business: write those psalms, stack them in a doll or in a tiny cushion, and sell them for protection."

"Simon declared, 'I cannot sell the house now. I spent too much money remodeling it. The market is down. I will lose money. I must find a way to get whatever the spirit is out of my life.' Denise suggested, 'Why don't you get rid of Ellie? She is probably part of the problem. She is an alley cat. Maybe she harbors an evil spirit. Don't you ever think of that?' Simon said, 'No, no, no, I can't live without Ellie. If I give her to the shelter, they are going to put her to sleep.' And then Simon burst into tears."

Tyler commented, "It is true. I have a cat. I love my cat. I could not stand the idea of giving him up, knowing that he would be put to death because he is old and not likely to be readopted."

Jose continued, "Denise told Simon that he should straighten up his life. His mother would not be proud of the way he is living. No children, no wife, going from woman to woman. She told him that he should keep his house clean like his mother had taught him. She also reminded him that he is at high risk of getting an STD. She stated, 'Brother, you are walking with your coffin under your arm. If you don't change your way of life, you will get HIV. If my mother could see you, she would be furious. Now, I know a woman who does house cleaning. I am sending her to clean your house. Let me know when you want her to come.' Simon answered, 'She can come every Friday.'

Denise gave Simon's house key to the housekeeper. Her name was Lydia. On a Friday morning, Simon already left for work when she arrived. She opened the door and went upstairs to look at the whole house. She met Ellie who started meowing. Her eyes turned red. She opened her mouth wide and sounded just like a feral cat, then gradually, she swells up and turned into a much bigger animal right in front of Lydia. Since the front door was not locked yet, Lydia ran down and made a quick exit in fear, screaming, 'Help! Help! The cat has turned into a tiger.' A neighbor who heard the scream called the police who arrived promptly to assess the incident. They went into the house. The cat was quietly laid on her bed. Lydia explained to the police what happened. They made a report according to what Lydia said. However, they couldn't take any action against Ellie. There was no evidence that the cat had turned indeed into a tiger.

Lydia did not have a chance to clean. She related what happened to Denise who believed her. Then, Denise called her brother to explain the incident. When Simon came home, the house was spotless, everything was in place, and even his bookshelf was put in order. All books were arranged in an orderly manner just like his mother used to do. She was very meticulous. Once again, his mother's favorite fragrance embalmed the house and most of all, his bible that was on the bookshelf was now placed on his bedside table. Simon has not touched a bible for years. Then, he felt that he has a problem or even two: the ghost of his mom and Ellie. He asked himself, 'Who is Ellie?' Then, he remembered that one evening, he had a woman in bed with him. Ellie came to his room and jumped on the bed, got feral, and scratched the woman who was a prostitute. She got dressed fast and said, 'I am out of here. Pay me please. Next time, come to my place, lover boy. I do not fool around with a cat.' At the time, Simon didn't make too much of it, but following that incident, he finally concluded that Ellie is part of his problem just like Denise said. And the question is what is he supposed to do?

The phone rang, it was Denise asking Simon if he has a living will or power of attorney. Denise said, 'Do you know that death is the only thing that is certain in life? It's a given.' Simon angrily replied, 'I am already stressed out and you are asking about my will. You are thinking about death. Why, what is the matter with you?' Denise replied, 'I am not asking you to think about death. I am telling you to prepare for it. Whether you think of it or not, it will happen. Because death is never late, it always comes, sooner or later. You have no family on your own. So, your siblings will be responsible for your funeral and all.' Simon shook his head saying, 'I can't believe what I am hearing. Do I have a death sentence, Denise? I see why your husband left you. Should I remind you that I am the eldest in the family?' Denise, upset, replied, 'You are the eldest, but you don't act like it. You think you are a teenager. You are not. It is time to grow up, Simon.' She hung up.

Simon called her back to tell her that Lydia's money is there. She can come to pick it up. She deserves to be paid. It was not her fault. She was attacked. Simon was facing a dilemma. Should he get rid of the cat or should he sell the house and keep the cat?"

Eli made a comment, "He should give the cat away because the spirit of her mother is embodied in the cat."

Jose continued, "Simon had a dream. In his dream, Ellie came to him as a person with his late mother's personality, mannerism, and voice, telling him that she is leaving. Because Simon is an awful sinner, when he dies, he will meet the devil in the atmosphere, and the devil will turn him into a pig and send him back to earth. 'I am your mother. God did not accept my soul because I was not a good person. I made other people around me miserable: your father, my mother-in-law, my stepchildren. I was overly critical of others. I was not generous. I cheated on my taxes all the time. It seems that God took note of that too, and I should know better. Jesus stated once, "Give to Caesar what belongs to Caesar." My soul was sent to wander around, so, the devil picked me up and sent me down to earth as a miserable cat. Do not let what happens to me happens to you, son. Every weekend, you have a different woman in your bed right in front of me. You are a real fornicator. You will be a pig one day. I am going away for good because I need to be redeemed somehow. I cannot live here any longer. Do not sell your house on my account. Goodbye, Simon. Oh, one more thing, give me your bible.' Simon all shaky said, 'Go get it.' Ellie said, 'How dare you. You must hand it to me, so you won't say that I stole it. Be more respectful of others. I am your mother, remember.'

When Simon woke up, his room was chilled, he was bewildered, and he couldn't believe what he dreamed of. He went to Ellie's room. She was not there and the bible was gone. Simon kept that experience to himself knowing that no one would believe him. Ellie left. Simon was saddened, but everything went back to normal. The end."

Everybody clapped for Jose, saying, "Great story, man. A lot to learn about the supernatural." "Too bad for those who don't believe in nothing," said Tyler. John added, "They will be a cow someday." Errol said, "The sister knew what she was saying when she told him that the cat is probably harboring a spirit. He is older, but the sister seems to have more experience." Eli said, "Women tend to be a little bit more clairvoyant than men though. That's my opinion." Omar declared, "Coming back to earth as an animal is a doctrine found in Buddhism and Hinduism. Islam, Judaism, and Christianity do not teach reincarnation."

CHAPTER 3

"I don't like his sister, Denise. Why go on and on talking about death and will? It reminds me of the time when I was in the hospital. A young nurse entered my room and said in a very distinct voice, 'Good morning, Mr. Calloway. My name is Susan, and I am going to be your nurse today. Do you have a living will, or have you given someone power of attorney?' I replied, 'An attorney! Am I locked up here?' She replied laughing, 'Oh no, basically, a living will is to let your loved ones know what you would like to be done for you if you ever become incapacitated.' 'Incapacitated! Why would I become incapacitated in a hospital?'

'If you do not have a living will, you can designate someone as your advocate, a person who will make the decision for you in case you are not competent enough to do so. Now, would you like to fill out a DNR form?' she spoke. 'What is that?' I inquired. 'DNR stands for do not resuscitate,' the nurse replied."

And Calloway stated, "'Take the N off the DNR. I want to be resuscitated. Do not let me die. You understand?' 'Very well, Mr. Calloway. We will make you a full code. I will let your doctor know,' she declared. 'Who is my doctor?' The nurse replied, 'Dr. Jude Hartley.' 'Why can't I have Judy or Judith, Juliet? I would much rather have a female doctor. As a matter of fact, I would like only females involved in my care. Female social worker, female nurse assistant, female lab tech, female drug and alcohol counselor,' Alloway requested. 'You are very funny, Mr. Calloway,' Susan replied pleasantly."

Tyrone said, "Mr. Calloway, what is your problem with male, if I may ask?" Calloway replied, "I have seen too many males in the service in Vietnam during the war." Someone said, "You are a Vietnam vet?" He answered, "Unfortunately, yes, I went to hell." And another voice said, "And fortunately, you came back." Everybody laughed. Omar said, "Calloway, do you have a living will or a testament now?" He answered, "Why should I? I don't care about what happens after I am gone." Eli asked, "What did you go to the hospital for?" "I did not go. I was taken by the paramedics who found me unconscious in the street, intoxicated. I was sent to detox after I was revived," he declared.

After lunch, Tyrone and Eli were spotted together. John commented, "Are those Eli and Tyrone together over there? Those two don't get along. What are they saying to each other? I hope Eli won't get into a fight with Tyrone." Tyler said, "Those two seem to know each other."

Tyrone went to tell Eli not to reveal their relationship, "Stepfather, why didn't you use your undergarment when you were going out to save yourself from embarrassment? What was the matter with you? Peeing in the park, and which park?" Eli replied, "Central Park East, in Manhattan." "O my God! Of all the parks, you chose a park in the heart of New York City, a predominantly white neighborhood." "What should I have done, urinate on me, like I am incontinent? What about you? Why are you here?" asked Eli.

Tyrone replied bashfully, "I was making out with my girlfriend in my car and a stupid cop spotted me." Eli laughed and said, "Why didn't you go to a motel? What was the matter with you, screwing someone in your vehicle? Do not say that you are my stepson and I raised you. Stepson and stepfather both locked up for indecency. We cannot be proud of that. So, let us be strangers for now. Don't you agree?" And Tyrone muttered, "As you wish, but should I remind you that black men and police do not mix? You are lucky you still have your penis intact." "See you around," Tyrone said loudly.

John said to Tyrone, "You and Eli seem to get along fine now. Is he preaching you about God, making you regain your faith?" Tyrone replied, "It is not that I do not believe in a supreme being. I hate religions altogether. My mother made me resent religion because she pushed me too hard into it. When I liberated myself from my family, I was freed from all religious doctrines. I don't believe in trinity. I don't believe in baptism to be saved because John the Baptist said, 'I baptize you with water, but the one who will come after me will be greater than me. He will baptize you with the holy spirit.' Men still do not understand. You must immerse yourself in the water to be safe. Where is Jesus Christ's baptism? Did Jesus ever immerse anybody in the water? No."

John declared, "I am not exactly a religious person, but I strongly believe in God. However, I do not believe in the Trinity doctrine. To me, God was, is, and will always be holy and a spirit. So, why is holy spirit an entity by itself?" Tyrone said, "Yes, why is that?" Tyrone continued, "Jesus is the most misunderstood figure that ever lived. Some said he is the second person of the trinity. In fact, Jesus is the first creation of God almighty. Jesus is the only one who has ever represented God on earth, not the pope. He was the messenger sent to teach mankind how to live and worship God."

John said, "Some declared that Jesus was not divine. What do you think of that, Tyrone?" He answered, "He had to be divine to interact with God, to understand him well, and he had to be human to understand and relate to mankind." "So, he was God then," said John. Tyrone said, "To us, humans, he was God because no man could not and had ever done what he did (bring Lazarus back to life and then bring himself back to life) so for us, he was God. But to God our Father, Jesus is Jesus, and it is as simple as that. Muslims and Jews claimed they can go straight to God without an intermediate. Seriously, I found that opinion somehow pompous. It's like telling me that you can see any president, any king, or the pope by just walking to their office and talk to them." John smiled and said, "No, even a mayor, you need someone to make the contact for you to see him face to face. So, it is the same for God, and remember, Tyrone, we were created in God's image. Some powerful men behave like they are God." Tyrone has a visitor, so, John said, "Nice talking to you, brother. You are no atheist, man, you understand. Peace! And see you around to hear some more stories." They split.

A new inmate arrived. He was a very tall and heavy man, looking like a wrestler but very arrogant. He looked around and see some other inmate reading. He declared, "I don't want to hear about God or the bible. No singing nor talking about Jesus or Christ. I am the Messiah, the only one the world would ever know." The inmates looked at each other and murmured, "He is a real schizophrenic with a delusion of grandeur. Watch out." Then, he asked, "Do you know who I am? I am Nero, the great Roman emperor. I am also the greatest gladiator that ever lived. If I put my hands on you, you would no longer need a lawyer because you would cease to exist. Do you understand me?" The prisoners together with a high-pitched voice ironically replied, "That is, *if*." He went berserk. He stretched his large arms, showing his muscles, saying, "I find you defiant and downright impertinent. What do you mean by 'If'? Why don't you step forward to show your face?" Another prisoner yelled sarcastically, "Why don't you step aside and backward?" He screamed, "Who are you?" Since he was getting too agitated and sounded violent, he was escorted away from the area by a prison guard.

Tyrone was scheduled to see the judge in a few days. He met with Eli to tell him the news, then he learned that Eli chose to remain in jail instead of going home—in part because he is lonely, he does not want to pay the utility bills, it is winter, and it is cold. So, he much rather spends the season in jail. Tyrone was surprised by his answer and his attitude about his situation, so he asked him, "Are you losing it? You want to spend your winter in jail, so you would not pay your rent or your bills. What is going through your mind?" Eli murmured, "Don't worry about me. I did that before. I will be fine. I can convert some prisoners to Christianity here." "Oh, great, what a great excuse, a missionary in jail. Did you just hear what that lunatic said?" Eli replied to Tyrone. "He is a lunatic. He will be transferred to a psych ward," Tyrone declared. "In this case, I have to tell your daughter. I have no other choice."

Eli begged Tyrone, "Don't tell her now. She has enough on her plate." "Is she in trouble? I have the right to know. She is like a sister to me," Tyrone declared. Eli said, "Let me rephrase it, she has some concerns. Allow her to be the one to confide in you." Tyrone answered, "No matter how you rephrase it, something is wrong, and I must find out what it is." Eli said, "It's about her grandchildren." "What about them? Are they sick or missing?" Tyrone questioned. Eli replied, "No, Grace was trying to find out more about the children's father." "Yes," said Tyrone. Eli continued, "Then, she had their DNA tested. Well, well." Tyrone interrupted, "Why do you keep saying well? What does the DNA reveal?" "The result is complicated and even shocking," declared Eli.

"What do the results say?" asked Tyrone. Eli answered, "I don't know and I don't want to know." "Really!" said Tyrone. "And how do you know it is shocking? First, Grace should not trust those commercially advertised DNA labs. Secondly, what could be so shocking? Maybe the two children are only half-siblings; meaning, they have different fathers." Eli smiled and said, "How could that be? They are fraternal twins. Have you forgotten?" Tyrone replied, "I have not forgotten. I have read about a case like that before. Don't you know that a white woman gave birth to two girls? One is white; the other is black. How surprising is that? Science cannot even explain it. So, I cannot think of anything worse than that." Eli said, "The children's father is a priest." "Right! You are so religious. Even your jokes are religious. A priest! That is a heavenly case! You made it up. You just said you did not know." Eli ignored Tyrone's remarks and kept talking, "My daughter made so many sacrifices to raise those children. She spent so much on them and now . . ." Tyrone said, "What are you trying to say? She spent money on her grandchildren. What's the big deal? These days, grandparents have full custody of their grand. I got to go now. Will finish talking later."

Eli was afraid of the awful truth about the children who now are teenagers. Grace did not know how to tell them that she is not their biological grandmother and that Lauralee is not their mom either. She has been raising them since they were toddlers as foster children. She was encouraged by the children's lawyer to adopt them. So, they would not go back to foster care or be adopted by strangers. She adopted them since the mother is disabled and there is no father around. Now, a test reveals that the children are not related to Lauralee, Grace's daughter. The DNA tests were performed by experts.

As for Eli, he is having a second thought about staying in jail for ninety days when he heard the voice of Vince McLaren, the mentally ill man inmate, screaming, "I can crumble you with my bare hands. I am a gladiator," while beating his chest. Someone commented, "Why is he still here? This guy needs his medicine, man! Or put him in a straitjacket."

While Tyrone was in court, Grace came to visit Eli Davenport, her father. Grace said to him, "I cannot believe you are behind bars again. Why, dad?" That is the second time, and about the same season. "Are you declining mentally, dad? Here is a problem. You are a Christian, a preacher. So, you should be a model citizen, not someone going in and out of jail. What can you possibly preach then?"

"I need you now more than ever. I have been looking for Tyrone. Have you seen him?" Eli hesitated and nodded, "Yes, I have seen him." Grace said, "Where is he at? I called him. I left a message. It's not like him not to get back to me." Eli said, "Eventually, he will call you back. He is okay. He is around." "Did he come to visit you?" Eli replied firmly, "Yes, he has."

Grace said, "If he comes to visit you, tell him about my situation. Dad, the story is unfolding. I have more information and what I found out is mind-blowing." Eli asked anxiously, "What did you find out?" Grace replied, "I hired an investigator to find out about that Catholic priest. His name is Jerome Solomon. He was not a priest at the time the children were conceived. He was a social worker student doing his externship in a woman shelter. According to the report, at the time, he was going out with a girl named Melody Brown. Coincidentally, Melody Brown gave birth to fraternal twins at the same time as Lauralee at the same hospital. They were on the same maternity ward. What do you make of that, dad?" Eli said, "Are you thinking what I am thinking?" "Spell it out, dad," Grace said.

Eli said, "Lauralee's babies were switched at birth? Unbelievable!" Grace replied, "I believe that's what happened. Wrong babies were given to Lauralee. I bet you Melody has Lauralee's children and I have Melody's children. I need a lawyer. By the way, dad, who is your lawyer?" Eli said, "I don't have a lawyer." Grace replied, "A public defender should or will be assigned to you, dad. You always need a lawyer, especially when you break the law." Eli asked her, "What are you going to do next?" Grace replied, "Get you out of jail, and now, let me finish. I did some digging on my own. Melody Brown does not live far from me. One day, I stopped by her house. I dropped an

Avon book with my phone number. She called me and asked me to pick up the book. She had ordered some cosmetics." Eli said, "You are kidding, right?" "No, dad, I am not, so I went back to get the book. One of the girls came out to give it to me. Dad, I had goosebumps. The girl looks exactly like Lauralee when she was a teenager. I took the book and I said, 'You remind me of my daughter. Would you give me a hug?' She came and embrace me, and as I was leaving, the mother came out to say thanks for the book." Eli demanded, "So, in that case, what is your next move?" Grace replied calmly, "My next move, dad, I am going to sue the hospital for negligence, and it is going to be a big case. I am going to sue their ass."

Eli said, "What are you after, money? Or are you ready to exchange the children? You are emotionally attached to those children. Now, would you be willing to let them go and take the other children you do not know? You need to do a lot of thinking before acting. A lot is at stake here. The children on both sides will be affected. Talk to Tyrone and listen to what he has to say on the matter because this is a very delicate and complex situation. How Lauralee will react, she is mentally unstable. Tyrone will get in touch with you soon and he will tell you where he is staying. To tell you the truth, I would leave it alone because you love Gina and Farrah so much.

Would you have the heart to let them go?"

Grace replied, "I know that, but the truth also hurts, to be alive and knowing that your children, your blood, would never know who you are." Grace was crying hard. Eli got close to her to comfort her. "Don't cry, don't despair. God will show you what path to take. You must seek God, Grace. You must call on him in your moment of need. He will direct you. Believe me, he will. Do not think much about making money by suing the hospital. If you are begging God to take on your case, do not get money involved. Let God decide what is good for you. You are not rich, but you are not poor either. You are happy with your grandchildren who love you very much." Grace said, "Dad, how would you feel if you know that your child is living with someone else and will never get to know you?" Eli replied sadly, "I don't want to think about that."

Tyrone returned. Eli filled him in on what is really going on with Grace and the grandchildren. In desperation to find a solution, the two decided to expose the problem to the other inmates to see what will come up. So, they organized a round table where each person had a say on the subject. Tyrone exposed the case. Eli said, "For the sake of each party in question, the grandmother should leave it alone because that is going to create a lot of confusion for the youngsters." Calloway raised his hand and said, "Eli, as a man, you can do that, but a woman would not let go. She will go insane, fully aware that her grandchildren will never acknowledge her and she is taking care of someone else's children. No, no, man. This must come out somehow. I am telling you." Tyrone said, "Thank you for your input." "You're welcome," Calloway replied. Errol raised his hand and stated, "In my opinion, the best thing to do is to let it go for now until the children reach eighteen. Then, the grandmother will bring the situation to the other mother who has her children. They should settle the case between them quietly. At eighteen, they are legally adult. They can choose their parents."

Tyler said, "I have heard of a case like that before. Everybody involved will be affected. One way or another, it's not a clean cut. Firstly, the grandma cannot sue the hospital unless she had power of attorney from her disabled daughter. Now, I assume she is an older woman. The real mother is disabled. With young people, you do not know what to expect. Are they going to be compassionate for someone they do not know and who is invalid, meaning the real mother? Will they choose the grandmother over the other woman they have known all their lives as their mother? I doubt it. Teenagers can be ruthless, and if or when that happens, the grandma will be crushed, feeling rejected. So, think carefully before acting." "Thanks, man, your point is well taken," said Tyrone. Jose said, "Should not she contact a lawyer for guidance? She cannot do it on her own."

John said, "Once a lawyer gets involved, the case will be wide open to the media. Reporters will want to talk to her and remember, lawyers mean money. They want money. Do you need them or not? No going around the bushes. Do you want him to help you get your grandchildren or not? And if you hire one, the case will be no longer a secret. Social worker will be involved. Hospital or foster home where the children spent the first years of their lives all must answer some questions. The media will take over. The case will be on TV. I guarantee you that."

Omar said, "May I say something? The grandma should establish a relationship with the other mother, I mean become friends, and make her talk, tell her what happens, that the children's DNA does not match her daughters' and see her response to that. Let her know about the father. She will have a reaction, and that will prompt her to have her children's DNA checked also. I bet you because the name of the father will bring a cloud of doubts about the children."

"Thank you all for your input. It means a lot to me," said Tyrone. Calloway said, "Is that person related to you?" Tyrone said, "Yes." "Well, good luck to you, bro!" said Calloway. Finally, John said, "Look at how Tyrone and Eli get along. Why do I have the feeling you two have a connection? I am just joking. It crosses my mind. What has happened? Tyrone is no longer an atheist." Eli replied, "He is alright." Tyler said, "Phil, you are the one who asked for stories to help keep your mind off of your problems. Don't you have any story to tell us? We would like to hear from you."

"How about you? You did not say anything," Phil replied. Tyler said, "I serenaded you with my accordion. We sang along, remember?" "Oh yeah," said Phil.

CHAPTER 4

Phil uttered, "One day, a woman was passing through a park. On a bench, she saw a red designer duffle bag. She looked around, did not see anyone, and picked up the bag. She could not open it because it was locked. She carried it home anyway. Her husband was a straightforward man. He asked her what that is. She replied, 'Don't you see what it is? It is a bag. I found it on a bench in the park.' The husband said, 'I want you to take it back where you found it.' The wife said, 'Okay.' But she went to her mother instead with the bag. There, she broke it open.

The content of the bag was a hammer, a pair of scissors, a black doll, a compressed black pack of a white powder she believed to be cocaine, and four thousand dollars in cash. She was thrilled, and her mother and sisters danced and rejoiced. The mother said, 'But what are you going to do with the cocaine? You should turn the whole pack to the police.' Nancy said, 'Are you out of your mind, mother?' She replied, 'No, I am not out of my mind, Nancy. I am contemplating you doing time in prison. Just give me some money. I would not partake in any drug activities. You can get life in prison for drug possession. Don't you know that?' 'Why should I be caught? People find treasures all the time. You are so negative. You don't take chance in anything at all. Don't you know, no pain, no gain, mom?' Nancy declared. Her sister Roberta said, 'Mom is right, Nancy. Why don't you place the drug in an old bag and take it to the police? Tell them exactly where you find it.' She replied, 'It's not that simple. They are going to make a report, ask me a lot of questions, my address . . . Bob told me to take it back to the bench. I let him know that I am going to, but I am not stupid.' Roberta said, 'I have another idea. Why don't you grab the money and take the bag back?' She said, 'Why can't I have it all? I can sell the cocaine to a dealer and make much more money.' Her sister, Angelina, said, 'O my God! You are blinded by the dollar sign. What good does it do to have money and be incarcerated for the rest of your life?'"

Calloway commented, "What a greedy woman! A super bitch!"

Phil resumed, "Nancy got upset. She left without giving any money to her mother and sisters. She went to the bank and made a deposit of one thousand dollars on her husband's account, one thousand on her son's account, and two thousand on her account. Then, she contacted a drug dealer to sell the drug. Unfortunately, the dealer, after testing the drug for purity, turned it down saying that the white powder is not cocaine at all and does not know what it is. Nancy, extremely disappointed, dumped it near a subway station trash can and watched a homeless man picking it up from the trash can. Then, she went back home with the bag. She hid it under her son's bed. Incidentally, Robert, her husband, who usually checked his bank account online daily noticed that a transaction has been made on his account. It's one thousand dollars, so he asked his wife if she knows anything about that. Nancy told him the truth. He was furious. He immediately removed the money from his account and put it on Nancy's.

Three days later, the headline on every newspaper was about the National Bank being swindled. Four thousand dollars turned into elm tree leaves. Nancy and her family were watching television when the news came on. She became edgy. That is her bank. That's the value she deposited. Robert shook his head in disbelief saying, 'That is my bank. Unbelievable! Everything is possible these days. Money turned into leaves. How about that?'

The next day, the FBI was at his door wanting to interrogate Nancy. The bank had traced the money to Nancy and her son Rick's accounts."

Omar commented, "I have never heard of that before. Money turns into leaves, so, leaves can be turned into money. What a trick!"

"I have heard of it before. That is black magic. Bob was right. He is not greedy. Otherwise, he also would be going to jail for fraud."

Phil continued, "After the interrogation, Nancy went to jail. Shortly after her arrest, there was an endemic of nosebleed, burned noses, swollen nostrils, and sore nose with exudate among drug users."

Tyler said, "I know the rest of the story. The homeless man sold the powder as cocaine and the powder was a strong chemical, a cutting agent." Phil said, "You got it right. Consequently, some people died of infection of the nose. Some drug addicts ended up having cosmetic surgery to fix their noses. Some others were walking around with half a nose."

The police came back to pick up the bag. The husband said he had no idea where the bag went. Only Nancy knew. So, Nancy was questioned about the bag. She said that it is under her son's bed, but her son does not know about it. Police went to pick it up. They got it from under the bed. They reported what was in the duffle bag—a hammer, a tall black doll with long hair, and a pair of scissors. The police confiscated the bag with all the content, but two hours later, the bag was nowhere to be found. It disappeared mysteriously. It was in the news: 'The police are looking for a red duffle bag. If anyone knows anything about the bag, please contact the police.' Drug users were also warned not to buy cocaine because there is poisonous cocaine going around.

Cocaine addicts could no longer trust their drug providers. Some went to rehab because they were afraid of using cocaine or any drug in powder form.

One night, Rick, Nancy's son, had the worse experience of the supernatural. It was around midnight when he went to bed. He was about to fall asleep when he heard a noise like someone is opening something, like a zipper, and he also felt a presence in his room. He got chilled. He closed his eyes and he changed side. He was petrified when he saw a black doll walking around his room. He screamed, but nobody heard him. His father was sleeping in another room. His sisters were next to his room sound asleep. The doll turned into a short woman with long hair and scary eyes. He watched her going to the safe and taking money and pieces of jewelry. She kept shaking her plump behind. Rick suddenly had an erection. He went to the motion of having sex with someone while he was alone. He closed his eyes, then he heard the zipping sound again. He opened his eyes and witnessed the doll going back into the red duffle bag. Finally, the bag levitates in the air and left the house. Then, his erection was over, and he was confused, numb, and disoriented till morning. He could hardly find a word to explain his experience to make it believable. Subsequently, he explained to his father what he went through. He understood and believed him because their money and their jewelry were missing. Moreover, the police reported that they found the bag with four thousand dollars, a pack of white powder, a hammer, a pair of scissors, and a tall white doll this time."

John said, "What's the big idea behind that duffle bag? I bet you. The police are going after the money and might even end up in jail too. Because money is tempting, four thousand bucks, everybody would want to try it before throwing it away thinking it is a green leaf."

"At this point, it was clear that the bag has supernatural power. The police were puzzled. No matter where they placed the bag, it will disappear and reappear somewhere else in town. In the end, the police commissioner recommended burning the bag and the money. They apparently did. However, some officers found a way to sneak some greens before burning the whole batch. The officers who took the money had an interesting supernatural experience. They all were walking around with an erection they could not explain. One of them learned of Rick's experience and finally concluded that he must burn the money he took. Before he did, the cash turned into green leaves right in front of him. One communicated his experience to the others and that was the end of the story."

"This is really spooky. So, these guys were walking around with their penis sticking up." Everybody laughed. "I would like that in bed, man, not at work." Calloway said, "Do you know that most of the guys coming from the war have ED or erectile dysfunction?" "Do you, Calloway?" asked Eli. "Well, you know, as you grow older, you can't stand up as you used to. Things change with age. That's why I am not interested in a young woman who requires a lot of moves. I cannot make those movements anymore. I have bad hips, bad knees.

I must be frank with you, I cannot do much sexually unless I take a sexual stimulant," admitted Calloway. Eli replied, "That is okay. We had our time. We cannot be young forever. We are not potent, but we are still important, aren't we?" "I suppose we are, bro," responded Calloway. Someone chuckled, "What does that mean not potent but important? I can't believe you guys. You don't keep that a secret?" Eli replied, "Why keep it a secret? Most men have this problem, especially those who are diabetic and those on some blood pressure medication. Sooner or later, son, you will experience erectile dysfunction. Enjoy your virility while you have it."

The storyteller continued, "Nancy is in jail. Bob felt ashamed and humiliated because his wife went to contact a drug dealer. He wondered how Nancy could know drug dealers. He had a lot of questions. Even though Bob was angry, he went to visit his wife in prison. Nancy, so embarrassed, refused at first to face him. Bob insisted on seeing her. Finally, Nancy accepted the visit. Bob said to her, 'I don't even know you anymore. Are you the woman I married? What made you do what you did?' Nancy hesitantly said, 'I needed . . .' Bob responded fast, 'No, it is not a matter of need, Nancy. You are simply driven by greed. I am not a rich man, but I am not exactly a poor man who cannot provide for his wife and family. I am a working man, and I am content with what I have. You are a stranger to me. I did not know you at all. Your mother and sister warned you about going to jail. You did not care. You are fearlessly determined to sell cocaine to drug dealers.' Nancy said, 'It was not even cocaine. It was some kind of . . .' Bob quickly added, 'Cutting agents. That does not make it less of an offense. You should not be dealing with cutting agents either. They are chemicals used to dilute recreational drugs.' Nancy said, 'Are you getting a lawyer for me, Bob?'

'Your son will take care of that. You almost messed up my life. Unfortunately, I still love you, and I do not even know why, and to tell you the truth, I do not like you right now. I am really distressed by the present situation.'

Nancy said, 'I am so sorry, Bob. You don't deserve that. I want to stay in jail. Let me do the time to pay for my mistakes and redeem myself.' Bob replied sarcastically, 'Oh, really! Your inmates will not play pat a cake baker's man with you. The world of prison is a tough world. Life in jail is by no means agreeable or desirable. You will not like your uniform, the rigid discipline, the humiliation from prison guards, and the overall treatment. Jail is not a boarding school, Nancy. So, reconsider your option, my dear. Will see you next week.'"

Errol asked, "So, Nancy was in jail, just like us. What was the charge exactly?" One person said, "Counterfeit money." Someone else replied, "How could it be?" Omar responded, "It is counterfeit because, before turning into leaves, it was fake money. However, she found it. She would not go to prison. As for the failure to return the money, a good attorney could easily argue that four thousand dollars are not that much money to return to the state." "That is right," said Eli. "Finders' keepers," Tyler said. "How about the powder?" Phil replied, "She was not charged for the powder. There was no evidence of any powder. It was never disclosed to the police."

Calloway commented, "I wish I know the magician who pulled that trick. If I had that money that can turn into leaves after forty-eight hours or so, I would spend it fast and I would not be caught." John asked smiling, "Where did you get that story, Phil? It is interesting. Did that really happen thus?" Phil responded, "Brother, I heard the story. I just repeat it. True or not, I do not know. A story is a story. By the way, guys, I have a court appearance tomorrow. I do not know if I will be back here or transferred to somewhere else. So, if I do not come back, this is goodbye, and thanks for the jokes, the stories, the sing-along. I will miss you all. God bless." "Good luck to you, Phil!" they all said.

At the Women Correctional Facility in Brooklyn, N.Y.

Nancy found some compassionate first-time offenders like her. A young woman approached her and spoke. "Hi! I am Ilda. You look scared, are you?" Nancy nodded, "Yes." And Ilda whispered, "Are you the lady with the money that turned into leaves? That could happen to anyone. Was somebody playing a joke? You should not be convicted for that. Don't you have a lawyer?" Nancy said sadly, "No, I don't want a lawyer." Ilda raised her voice to say, "You are a fool, girl. Life in prison is no picnic. Don't you have a family? What kind of game are you playing, woman? I want to get out of here so badly. And you, you want to stay in jail to redeem yourself. Do not repeat that again."

"You will change your mind in a couple of days," another woman came to her and spoke. "What did she tell you? Pay her no mind. She is a control freak. Do you have a private attorney? Do not count on public defenders. They will not do much for you." Nancy asked her, "What are you here for?" She replied, "I was delivering drug for a dealer and someone apparently called the police. I was caught with a pack of crack and some weeds. That's all." "I am sorry to hear that. By the way, what's your name?" "Millie," she replied and added, "My sister is getting me a lawyer because drug possession can be sometimes a misdemeanor or a felony. It depends." Nancy replied, "You should not be going to prison just for that." "Most likely, I will go." She sobbed, and Nancy saddened, then remembered her husband's advice, "Reconsider your option, my dear."

A woman in jail for battery got acquainted with Nancy. She asked her if she knows a shaman or a voodoo person who can accelerate her release. Nancy said no. She never contacted a voodoo priest or a magician in her life. Genesis asked, "How about the bag with the doll and the hammer?" Nancy explained that she found the bag placed on a bench in a park. Genesis asked her, "What made you pick up the bag?" Nancy claimed, "Because it was a brand-new designer duffle bag. I was more interested in the bag. I did not know what the content was. It was locked. I could not see what was inside. So, at home, I broke the lock and saw the money. My husband told me to take it to the police. I didn't." Genesis voiced, "Good, you do not listen to him. Why would you give the money to the police? Most men are like that. They want complete control over women. We cannot have money, we should be asking them, making us dependent on them. Fu . . . them all. Listen, I will tell you a story about magic, later. Hang in there, baby."

Nancy smiled and said, "Okay, I would like to hear it." Millie rushed to Nancy to murmur, "Genesis is a troublemaker. She beats up her husband's girlfriend. Do not say I told you."

Nancy then introduced herself to a young girl named Jennifer who reminds her so much of her daughter Kayla. She inquired why she is in jail. Jennifer told her that she stole her mother's computer and used her credit card to get cash for drug. Her mother turned her into the police. Nancy was heartbroken, thinking that could happen to her daughter and was filled with remorse for trying to sell drug to drug dealers. Thinking that her children also can succumb to drug addiction, she made the decision to join mothers against drug dealer's organization once she gets out of jail. She made a phone call to her husband begging him to hire a lawyer for her. She advised Jennifer to get help from drug rehabilitation, go back to school, engage herself in a good hobby like sport (tennis), music, something to keep her mind always occupied. Boredom can drive people to drug.

Genesis gathered her mates to tell them a story of magic because she strongly believes in it. She related the case of one of her relatives who had an absentee husband. He was working in another state. The relative was her second cousin. To assure that her husband does not mess around with another woman, she went to see a mambo, which is a woman practicing voodoo and magic. Millie asked, "Are magic and voodoo the same thing?" Genesis said, "No, voodoo had to do with worshipping spirits, mostly spirits of African ancestors. I do not worship anything. If I ever decide to worship something, it would be God, not the spirits of any African ancestors. What have they done to worship them? I find voodoo really stupid."

"However, the mambo can do magic. Any voodoo priest can do magic spells." Millie said, "Remember, Genesis, magic does not last. You know that, and sometimes, magic does not do anything at all. I have been there, I know." Genesis chuckled saying, "I know girl, I know. Listen to what happened to my cousin. She went to see the mambo, right. She asked what she can do to keep her husband not to have sex with other women but her even when he is away. The mambo requested that she brings her husband's sperm in a tube with one hundred fifty dollars to make him impotent while he is away from her. Linda, my cousin, managed to get the sperm." "How?" Ilda asked. "Well, simple. Her husband wears condom sometimes. She got it from the condom. She took it to the mambo who gave it back to her well-packed in another container and instructed her to put it in the freezer till her husband returns home and then to bring it back to her to reverse the spell. Linda did exactly what she was told. When he got back home, he was completely impotent. He told his wife something is wrong with him sexually because he has no sexual desire for the last three months. His wife next to him naked means nothing. He could not have an erection, or it will take him an hour to have one that lasts only a minute. He tried to watch pornography. Nothing excites him anymore. He was like a dead man, completely impotent. Apparently, Linda neglected one little detail—she should have taken the tube back to the mambo to reverse the spell. Instead, she threw it in the trash since her husband was home. She did not want him to see the tube in the freezer. He would ask what that was." Nancy stated, "Maybe it was not the sperm in the freezer having any effect at all. Instead, her husband was probably low in testosterone, the major sex hormone in men. He needed to see his doctor who would have prescribed him some testosterone shots every month or so. There was nothing magical there."

Genesis said, "Till now, he never regains his virility. He needs to take a pill to get an erection." And she laughed. Millie said, "Is there any truth in placing the sperm in the freezer? Maybe it does work. It simply backfired. Linda can no longer enjoy her husband as she would like to. I have learned one thing in life, ladies. You should not go to the extreme for anything."

Nancy said, "Jennifer, you are so quiet. What do you think of that story?" She replied with a smile, "I can't say magic works or doesn't work. It has been around for so long. There must be some truth to it, I suppose. I think, in Linda's case, it backfired. She should have gone back to the magician to have whatever was done before reversed." Genesis agreed with Jennifer and added, "I would like to know how to turn green leaves into money. That is the work of a genius. I heard that happened before, in Haiti. But you know what? Magic does not last thus. We all remember our childhood tale of Cinderella. The chariot would turn into mice and clothes into rags. At midnight." "Oh yea, that's right. There is a frame of time given for the spell to work."

Simone, another inmate, joined the group, "Hey, ladies, I heard your stories. I like stories about the supernatural. I like fantasies and mystery. May I join you? My name is Simone. I originally come from Capernaum, US, not from Israel. It's a remarkably interesting city." Jennifer said, "Tell us a story, Simone." She replied, "I don't have a spooky story to tell." "Tell us anything. We are telling stories just to keep our minds off the prison, making the hours more pleasant."

Simone related, "There was a man who was mentally disturbed. I do not mean to say he was all crazy. Because he was an educated man, once a high school teacher, he had a home, but he was a hoarder who chose to live in the street. You got to see his place, crowded with all kinds of junk. Each month, he called himself a different name. His real name was Francis Lyons, but he called himself by different biblical names most of the time. He could be Abraham one day and the next day, he was John the Baptist. Quite pleasant he was, talking about the bible on and on. He made predictions that never come to pass. So, people ignored him and paid no more attention to his predictions. Seemingly, that was part of his mental disturbance. However, one day, he was leaving town. He had his backpack on his back and he spoke, 'Fellow citizens, a hurricane is coming our way. It's a category five. Be ready to swim or drown. The best you can do is to leave while you can. This town will be hit hard. God asked me to make a boat. I cannot say, "No God, I cannot make a boat." I do not know how Noah did it. It takes an extraordinary man to accomplish such a daunting task. Because me, first, I am afraid of fierce animals. How will the lions, tigers, panthers, lynx, jaguar, and puma get along with the other animals? Second, I would never put nasty creatures such as bedbugs, roaches, mice, rats, locusts, and such in the boat. They are a nuisance to men. Why save them? I want them destroyed. So, I rather skip town. I am Noah, but I cannot make an ark. God would understand.

To all of you, my math students, I am sorry. You will have to find the value of X on your own. Remember, what you do on the left, you do on the right. What you do in the east, you do in the west; what you do in the north, you do in the south. One more thing, remember to always reduce your fraction to the lowest term. If you do not, you will get an F. That is right. F like in failure, fake, fool, frack, fork, and fucking. I hope to see you again, maybe in another town, another time, or in another realm. Till then, farewell folks.'

A couple of weeks later, it started raining and the forecast said my town will be gravely affected by the hurricane. It was raining all day, all night, nonstop. Before we know it, all residents were asked to leave town. My aunt was in a retirement facility. She asked my mother to pick her up. My mother did not return to see her thinking that the facility would make an arrangement for her safety. It was not the case. My aunt perished in the flood. I was then a teenager. From the television, I saw my home destroyed and my stuff carried away by the water. I collected dolls and I saw them all floating on the dirty floodwater. My neighbors died. I could not save my dog and my cat because my family decided to leave at the last minute. I could not find them. They went on hiding. My mother could not get over my aunt's death. She carried the guilt with her to the grave."

"O dear, that is a sad story, but how about Noah?" asked Millie. "No one ever knew his whereabouts. He left, but his prediction lingers in my memory till today. I wonder, did God really send a message to him? How did he know, or was it just a guess?" declared Simone. Nancy responded, "No, Simone, he had a premonition this time because he left. He had never left and did not predict natural disaster before, did he?" "No, he did not."

"In the aftermath of the hurricane, Capernaum was renovated and became a beautiful, modern city with only one biblical feature, a city gate. As of now, it is the center of most Christian ministries because, as you probably know, the real Capernaum in Israel was Jesus' favorite town and the center of his ministry. I hope my story was not too boring for you," Simone added. The ladies responded, "You are kidding! That is a true and interesting story. It reminds us of hurricane Catherina. The kind of story that reminds us of how fast and easy it is to lose everything, even our lives."

Jennifer asked, "Simone, is it your first time in jail?" Simone said, "Yes." Then she explained, "I am here for disorderly conduct. I am pro-life, so I was part of a protest that went wild and some of us get arrested and I am one of them." Jennifer said, "You must be really pro-life to go out to protest."

"I was not always pro-life. I became pro-life, ladies. In that respect, I must make one thing clear. I am not a radical pro-life. There are instances when a woman has the right to terminate a pregnancy. We do know those circumstances, right? When I was just 18 years old, I found myself pregnant, and my boyfriend got mad at me for being pregnant. Right under my eyes, he went on with another girl who was much more attractive than I was. My friends encouraged me to get rid of his baby because he does not deserve to be a father. I resented him.

My parents did not know yet, and they would not agree to abortion because they were deeply religious. I planned the abortion. I went to the free clinic for it. On that day, the nurse who took all the information was the same nurse who came to prepare me for the procedure. She came with post-procedure literature to give me, but instead, she made me an offer. She said nicely, 'Your baby is well. Why do you want to murder him/her?' I was surprised. I opened my eyes wide and said, 'Murder!'

She said, 'Yes, Simone, that is what you are about to do. This child could be your meal ticket in the future, the best part of you, your only friend, your comforter that you want to destroy. Do not kill the baby. Have the baby and give him to me. When you are ready to take charge, I will transfer full custody to you with no fuss. You do not know what you are doing now. You will regret it later. It is not too late to change your mind. Do not sign the last paper I am presenting to you. I have five hundred dollars cash for you to start preparing for the birth of your son or daughter. Here is my card with my phone number. I am writing down my address. Call me anytime if you need anything. I have an organization behind me to support you, or if you decide to give up the baby for adoption, I will help you through the process. After birth, you will love that baby so much, you would not want me to have her/him. Believe me. However, if on the contrary, you feel bewildered, you do not know what to do, the offer still stands. I will be there for the baby.' Consequently, I did not go through with the procedure. I could not. I got dressed and left the clinic. This nurse was with me step by step for the duration of the pregnancy.

Her father was a real estate developer who had several buildings in Brooklyn. I was given a free apartment to live in for a year. I still live in the building. I rent a bigger apartment. My son is loving, so compassionate. He is my only child and without him, I would be so lonely. And two years after his birth, I was only 19 years old when I was diagnosed with endometriosis."

Jennifer asked, "What is that?" Simone explained, "It's when abnormal tissue grows outside the uterus and invades the ovaries and fallopian tubes. The doctor did a treatment that left me barren. So, you can understand why. I do not want other people to just go and have an abortion for no good reason."

"Well, you have a point. Look at you now. You cannot have another child. If you have had this abortion, girl, you would live with so many regrets. You would think that you have been punished by God," uttered Millie.

Genesis asked, "How did your family react to your situation?" Simone answered smiling, "Surprisingly, my father was my number one supporter and then my sister. My mother was so involved with the church. She hardly had time for us. However, after the baby was born, she came around. She was there for me, trying to help me get back on my feet and encouraging me to go to college, or to a vocational school, to get a skill. I love both my parents, but my dad is a real dad till now." Genesis said, "What is his name? I need a dad, now." Everybody laughed and Simone replied, "His name is Eli. I don't want him to know that I am in jail."

Ilda said, "Well, I see no reason for you to be here. You should be released soon. In recollection of that hurricane that destroyed Capernaum, my friend Fannie was living with her boyfriend Kaleb. They were about to get married. But Fannie suddenly had a change of heart. She did not want to make any commitment yet. She did not want to have children for him. Kaleb was not interested in children. He has a son, he hardly sees him, and he was not exactly a good father. So, Fannie wondered, will he be a good father for her child? Kaleb was a successful businessman. He was well off and Fannie is the kind of girl who likes luxury. She is a high-maintenance woman, and she loves sex. Kaleb had both: money and good sex. However, Fannie still was not fully satisfied. She missed romance in her life, affection. Every woman loves affection, romance, not just sex. We are not animals. Do not we all like a compliment, flowers, occasional surprise, not just money and sex? Some men are brutal. They are mostly after sex.

One day, before she got into that holy matrimony, she went to see a clairvoyant to tell her what lies in the future for her and Kaleb. When she got there, the woman presented a set of cards and told her to cut, meaning take half of the pile. She did and gave it to her. She read and said that she saw festivities. She is not sure what it is, and she said that she also saw a fish in the water, and she was smiling thinking she is giving her good news. Fannie stood up and said, 'What do you mean by fish in the water?' The psychic said, 'You have a baby on the way, you are pregnant, a baby boy. But I also see a bridge.' 'What does that mean?' Fannie inquired. She explained, 'Sometime in a near future, you and your son will be separated temporarily. Do not despair, Miss, everything will be okay. I am sorry to break with you what is forecast in the reading. That is what I see. Listen to the rest. Don't leave,' she begged her.

Fannie got upset telling the woman that she is lying. She paid her and left without listening to the rest of the omen. She did not like what she heard, but anyway, she went to a drug store, bought a home pregnancy kit, stopped at a department store, went to the bathroom, and did the test. It was positive.

Extremely disappointed, she told Kaleb who was very excited, and tried to cheer her up. Then, she called me and explained how she felt. I told her, 'You know, Fannie, you will not find all the qualities you desire in a person. Maybe it is time to teach Kaleb how to love his son with the other woman and to be more affectionate. Explain to him that being macho is not enough. A woman wants and needs attention out of bed too.' I told her not to be too difficult but to remember there is always another woman at the other end, ready to take her place. Fannie listened to me. They did get married on wedding days at Capernaum."

"What is that 'wedding days at Capernaum?" Genesis asked. "Two days in the last week of May are dedicated to marrying couples who have been living in a common-law relationship or anybody who wants to be married. It is a big event every five years. It is collective marriages where the whole town is invited. Christians got baptized in the river, missionaries, doctors, without borders, came to make miracles, homeless people are dressed and invited to eat, the city is responsible for decorations, a football field is arranged for the weddings to be performed, and there are a lot of visitors. It is a big event."

Ilda continued to relate, "Fannie and Kaleb got married later and they remained in Capernaum. Life was going well for them for years until the hurricane destroyed their dreams of raising a family together. All their possessions were gone. Fannie had watched Kaleb going into the flood water with her son Alexander. She was helplessly crying desperately to God to save her son and husband. Kaleb had Alexander and he was trying to hold on to a car, but the current was too strong. He fell in the water but someone with a life vest took Alexander. Kaleb swam away. Fannie fell into the water and almost drowned trying to rescue him. Fortunately, she was rescued and taken to a nearby hospital where she remained in a mental rehab ward for over a year. She was then discharged to a shelter. There she met other survivors of the hurricane. That is how I found her. I went to the shelter to volunteer and I was pleasantly surprised to see Fannie. She recognized me at once and we talked about Kaleb and her son wondering where they are. Did Kaleb and little Alexander survive?

Fortunately, we met a social worker who seemed to know where Alexander and other children were placed. He was helping Fannie in her search for her son, who was then placed in a foster home out of state. When the social worker got in touch with social services in Utah, he was dismayed when he learned that the boy was officially adopted and could not get any information about the family who adopted him. Fannie was heartbroken and slumped into another nervous breakdown. The social worker once again was there to help her recover.

In the midst of that, a romance developed between the two, but Fannie hesitated to get involved because a part of her still believed that Kaleb is probably alive, living somewhere. However, when a newspaper from Capernaum printed out a list of the names of victims, Kaleb's name appeared. So, Fannie lost hope and loneliness was taking a toll on her—no money, no child, no husband. When I asked her to come live with me, she said she will think about it. It did not take long for the social worker to take her home. He was a widower with one child, a little girl. Nothing could make Fannie whole again until she knows where her son was. Finally, she hired a lawyer to investigate the adoption."

CHAPTER 5

"**L**es Freeman, a lawyer from legal aid, took her case. Looking for the child in Utah, it was a dead end. The little boy adopted in Utah was a white boy with the same name and last name as her son, Alexander Harris." Nancy asked, "But where were you when the hurricane came on?" She replied, "I left town when they asked people to leave. I did not have a beautiful home or anything of value to be too sentimental about. I took a suitcase, and I was out of there. I am afraid of water. I do not know how to swim. My house is gone. I went to California to be with my sister. A lot of people perished because they love things. They are attached to things too much." Genesis said, "So, you went back to Capernaum after the flood."

"Yes," responded Ilda who continued to relate the story, "Fannie was invited by a minister to come to a revival. She went, and everybody was singing, praying, and when the time came for testimonials, a sister next to her said, 'Are you going to say something, sister?' Fannie replied coldly, 'What about? I lost everything.' And the woman replied, 'Except for your soul sister.' Fannie listened to all testimonials and decided not to testify since her faith was not the same. She had nothing to thank God for. Then, the minister said, 'Brothers and sisters, here are two boys: Williams Harris and his little brother Alexander Harris. Both were rescued by the Navajo Indians. They had lived in the reservation for three years. They are here with their mother Regina who found them. Regina is Williams's mother and Alexander is Williams's half-brother. Applaud. God is good. God is great. Amen'

'Sister Regina, come to the altar please.' Fannie was speechless. She did not even know what to do; she wept. Then, Regina took the microphone and testified how God is good. When she got a lead on the whereabouts of his son, she made to trip to the reservation. She found her son and was surprised that his brother was there with him. She had to pay a fee to take them with her. The place was like a boarding home. Parents who came to pick up their kids must pay or give whatever they can. She did not have enough money for both. She went on the street panhandling, begging, and got plenty to pay for both. She said she could not take her son leaving his half-sibling behind. Everybody shouted, 'Amen.' Fannie stood up to shout, 'Alleluia, praise God!' She burst into tears, crying so loudly the minister came to console her, find out her problem, and offered to help. Then, Fannie explained that she is the mother of Alexander and she knows Regina very well. She is a stepmother to Williams that she likes very much.

The two women met and embraced each other in tears, and they asked where Kaleb is. Fannie told Regina that a newspaper had listed Kaleb as dead. Regina asked about how they know that. He is not dead; he is missing. 'I cannot go look for him. He is your husband. I lost mine. I know that for sure. I saw his body. Now, it is your duty to go after Kaleb. If I were you, I would go to the state of Sonora in Mexico.' Fannie stated, 'You are sending me on a wild goose chase. Sonora is a state. I speak no Spanish at all. Where in Sonora is Kaleb?'

Regina uttered, 'Ask the pastor to help you. He has a ministry in Sonora to convert the Indians. He might know something. Somebody told me that Kaleb is probably working in the Indian territory in Mexico, teaching them how to read and write. And I am sure a Christian ministry is behind that. As I said, I cannot help you look for him.' Fannie said, 'Why is that?' She replied gently, 'Conflict of interest. He is an ex-lover.' Fannie declared, 'And the father of your son. Have you forgotten?' 'Still your husband,' added Regina.

'I have not told you yet how grateful I am for what you did for me. How can I ever pay you? You gave me back my faith in God. I felt that I was forgotten,' Fannie told her. And Regina replied, 'Do not feel bad. We all go to that phase in our lives when we wonder if God is really looking after us. You know he exists. You cannot doubt that, but does he really take care of us? That is the question. Well, I know you would do the same for Williams.' Fannie said, 'I will always be there for you and Williams, but now, if Kaleb is alive, why would he stay away?' Regina said, 'Does he know you are alive?' 'Not a reason for not coming back home,' Fannie responded."

Simone said, "Excuse me, may I say something? Remember, Kaleb is not a romantic or a sentimental type. He is probably not attached to anybody. Some men are like that. Once their sexual needs are met, they are fine. They are not like us women who care about family and children, all that." Everybody approved and said, "That's true."

Ilda continued, "Finally, Regina asked the minister if he knows a man by the name of Kaleb Harris who is teaching in a village of the state of Sonora. The minister replied that the name is familiar. He has many rescued from the hurricane in Mexico at the nearby border. He remembered marrying a man named Kaleb to an Indian girl. They were living together. As a minister, he encouraged them to get married. He had no idea that the groom has a wife who is alive. 'I am sorry for making such a mistake.'

He took an album and showed Regina the picture of new converts and newlyweds. Regina recognized Kaleb. It was him in a picture marrying an incredibly young Indian girl. Regina was in disbelief, not sure how to handle the situation. She reasoned, 'Not all truths are good to tell. In that respect, it is not my place to spell it to her. I do not know how she would react to that awful truth.' In the final analysis, she decided not to tell Fannie but discouraged her instead not to go to Mexico looking for Kaleb.

So, she told her that she was right at first. Looking for Kaleb in the state of Sonora is really like looking for a needle in the haystack. The Indians are not always friendly with American visitors, and moreover, she has a communication problem (she speaks no Spanish or the Indian dialect). Besides, she might be going for a big disappointment. To that, Fannie had replied, 'Disappointment is part of life.' Then, Regina pointed out to her that because she has a history of depression, she should not be looking for a trigger.

'If Kaleb is alive, he will find his way back home,' Fannie stated that as she is looking for peace of mind. She wants to be sure that Kaleb is dead or alive so she can go on with her life without any doubts or regrets. She wants to be free.

Fannie was determined to go to Mexico and she asked Regina to go with her. Regina refused, but when Fannie insisted and decided to go anyway with or without Regina, Regina accepted to tag along.

They went to Sonora, Mexico leaving the boys with me (Ilda). With the help of a tourist guide, they and a missionary traveled to the valley of the Rio Yaqui, in the Mexican state of Sonora, where Kaleb lived with his wife and a baby girl. Regina and Fannie arrived at the time of festivities when the Indians were getting baptized. It was a big event for them. Fannie and Regina were escorted to the village where the festivities took place after the baptismal. With a picture of Kaleb in her hands, Fannie was asking people if they know him. They all shook their head to say no, but one woman said yes (with gestures). She knows him. 'He is a teacher,' she said. 'Come, I will show you his house. Here, this is where he lives with Anacaona, his wife, and their baby girl.' Fannie said, 'Are you sure it is him?'

The woman nodded to say, 'Yes.' Fannie's face changed. Regina asked her if she wants to confront him face to face. Fannie said, 'No. Let us go peek at his house.' They went to his address, looked through, and saw him all dressed up in Indian attire, coming out with his wife and baby on their way to the party. He seemed healthy and happy. The wife was young and very pretty with exceptionally long and luxurious hair that covers her back entirely.

Courageously, Fannie said, 'Let us go back to the hotel. He is alive and well. I am happy for him. I would never disturb such a nice family—a young mother, a baby. So, goodbye, Kaleb. I had my time with you. Thank you, God, thank you, Regina. I come to Sonora, I see my husband, and I understand. Today is then, a new day. A new chapter in my life begins.'"

Everybody said, "Interesting story. It could happen to any of us." Genesis commented, "What a woman is Fannie! She is so cool!" One detainee said, "I agree with her." Another one said, "I would want an explanation." A voice said, "To make a fool of yourself. He is already taken by a much younger woman. Three years had passed. You are disconnected with each other. What are you going to do?" Jennifer said, "I would want answers. I could not leave without talking to him about the circumstances that led him to a carefree attitude. Is he a captive or an amnesiac? You never know. I find it hard to turn back not saying a word."

Nancy replied, "Different people handle things differently. Maybe they were not very emotionally connected. Remember, at the beginning of the story, she had a change of heart. She did not want to get married." Jennifer said, "O, yea! She got pregnant and then she was obliged to marry him. You are right, Nancy." A much older woman who hardly speaks made a comment, "He is not captive, a minister married him. There is more to love than just sex. Fannie loved this man a great deal. Most of you would not understand real love when you see it. The man seemed happy. He has a new family. If you love him, you must give him up. Because you love a man does not mean you must have this man to yourself." Jennifer replied, "How does she know he is happy? Appearance can be deceitful." The woman replied, "That is beyond her scope to assess."

"Upon their return, Fannie was greeted at the airport by Anthony Jenkins (social worker). Fannie, Anthony Jenkins, (social worker), Alexander, Nellie, (Anthony's daughter), and Meinecke (Nellie's dog) altogether formed a new nuclear family in Capernaum," Ilda recounted. Millie questioned, "How is it going to play out?" "What do you mean, Millie?" inquired Ilda. Millie explained, "It is going to be a legal knot for those people to be legally a family. Given the facts that her husband is alive, living in a foreign land, and not knowing if his wife is alive. That is why I think it was wrong for Fannie not to contact him at all. So, tell us, Ilda, how it ended." Ilda explained, "Fannie divorced him. It was a long process and a complicated case like you said, but it was done."

Nancy inquired, "How about Kaleb? Did he ever return to the state?" Ilda responded, "Kaleb was content. He lived a simple life among the Indians. He had lands, he even had a ranch, and he was then a farmer and doing very well. He came to visit his parents and his sons every two years and sometimes invited them over to Mexico.

That is all, ladies, life has different kinds of surprises." Nancy replied sadly, "Anything can happen and there is no way to prepare us for the unexpected. Look at me in jail. I want to get out of here. I miss my family."

Millie suddenly began to speak, saying, "I had the chance to meet a nice couple with two sons, Albert and Norman. They were two gentle adolescents, very respectful, doing well in school. Albert was always teasing his younger brother Norman calling him name, a name that infuriated him (sissy) because Norman at an early age was girlish and that worried their parents. They did all they could to make him act more like a boy, encouraging him more in men-oriented activities such as boxing, karate, and wrestling for youngsters. Norman had little or no interest in any of those activities.

He was a sweet boy who adored his mother. He loved drawing. He designed a skirt for his mother when he was only ten years old. The mother, Lois Benton who was a seamstress, made the skirt and received many compliments for it.

The father, Roger Benton, was pushing him hard to be and look like a tough boy. He even sent him to Nigeria in a group vacation to learn how to play the drum during the summer vacation in Africa."

Nancy interrupted to comment, "I know where the story is going. The parents were trying to change his sexual inclinations, but it is a lost battle. Norman was born with a defect. Nothing was going to change that. I have seen a case like that in my family."

Millie continued, "One day, the big brother called him and spoke to him harshly saying, 'Everybody is talking about the way you talk. You better change. You will not be gay. We do not want gay in the family. Do you understand? If you decide to act on your feeling, you should evaporate, disappear. Don't stay in this town. It will be a disgrace for our family.' Norman replied, 'What gives you the idea that I am homosexual?' Albert answered, 'The way you talk, walk, your mannerisms.' Norman replied, 'If that is the case, I am born like that. So, there is nothing I can do about that, Al.'

Albert said, 'I love you, brother, except I do not like homosexuality because I do not understand it. It does not make sense to me.' Norman added, 'And the bible punished those who practiced it, right?' Al replied, 'No, not at all. I do not think what happened to Sodom had to do with homosexuality only. The inhabitants of Sodom were inhospitable, unwelcoming toward people. They were bad folks, living in these two cities, who had no regard for God and the laws. Besides, Sodom and Gomorrah were nothing in comparison to what is going on now. There are no sanctions from God nor from the state. Homosexuality is legal. If it is considered a sin, it is not an ordinary one, but one with a license. Let me tell you, Norman, you are my brother, the only brother I have. I can never reject you. If you ever feel that you must become a homosexual, do not defend homosexuality. Accept that it is wrong, but you cannot help it because you are probably born this way. It happens to people. The hormones are perhaps mixed up, not the right ones for boys and that makes you feel like a girl. Nevertheless, that does not make homosexuality right and acceptable. Think about it, if the first humans were two men or two women, you and I would not exist today. The world would not be populated at all. In this regard, we, humans, are much more intelligent than animals, yet a male dog is not attracted by another male dog. They do not mate. At least I have not seen that yet.

So, if animals do not do it, why do we, humans, do it? I am afraid that sooner or later, brother, you might feel attracted by another man. You probably will not be able to fight it. Simply pray on it, ask God to intervene. Remember I will always be your brother. I will welcome you to my home with open arms, but I will not welcome you under my roof with a male lover. I am sorry. I would rather pay for a hotel room for you and that you will understand and forgive me.'

Norman replied, 'It seems that you have my future in the palm of your hands, brother. You are so sure that I am gay. Frankly, I must confess that I would feel much more comfortable being a woman because I am not comfortable in my own skin as a man. Nevertheless, I have no desire for another man, at least not yet. Since you seem to know a lot, Albert, what scientific studies said about my case, help me to be more man. Please do.' Albert timidly responded, 'All I told you is from me. I have not read any scientific research on the subject. I am just guessing what could probably make you feel like a woman. You have been like that since you were little. You feel like a woman. Maybe someday, you will be a woman. Who knows you will follow those men who turned themselves into women? Only God can judge them.'"

Genesis asked, "Did Norman turn gay for real?" Millie replied, "Norman went to college to become a social worker. He never came back home. He was living in Texas at one time. He used to call his parents and wrote to them, send money to his mom sometimes, and then, all contacts stopped. Lois had never heard of Norman. Roger died. Norman never knew if his father passed since they did not know his whereabouts. Lois was distressed. A son that she loves so much forgot all about her. With Roger gone, Albert took a job overseas, Lois was alone, her house was repossessed, and she had little to live on. Then, the worse happened, she was becoming blind due to an eye disease called macular degeneration." Ilda said, "O wow, this macular degeneration is worse than glaucoma. My aunt and my grandmother had it."

Genesis commented, "It is like an ordeal for a mother when a son, daughter, or husband is missing, when you don't know where to turn or who to turn to." Nancy said, "In a case like that, you cannot even go to the police. He is not considered missing. He stopped all contacts with the family." Ilda said, "Remember, the brother told him to evaporate if he became a homosexual; he did. Albert was bullying him. He does not want his parents to know what kind of life he is living. He is alive, I guarantee you that. People can stay away for fifty years or more."

Millie continued saying, "Albert rarely wrote or called his mother, and one day, Lois told me, 'You know, I regretted not having a daughter. If I had a daughter, I would not be so lonely.' Then, one day, I took her to the social service office. There, she found some help. She was sent to live with a woman as a border. My parents had sold their house, so, we moved to another vicinity. I did not see Lois for a few months. I did not know where she was. Social service would not give me her address. She was no longer a border. I tracked down the woman who oversaw the boarding home to find out where Lois went. She kindly gave me her address and mentioned that her daughter came to pick her up."

Everyone listening had a comment. "I bet you it's Norman who had become Norma," one of the inmates said. Millie explained, "I was shocked. I know she had no daughter. I did not think of Norman at all. I went to the address. It was a beautiful house. Lois was sitting on the porch. I said, 'Lois, it is me, Millie, do you remember me?' 'O, how could I forget you, Millie, my youngest friend? How is your mom? Does she still go to the casino? I miss the good old days when we used to hang together and have a good time. How is everything going for you, Millie?' I answered and I asked her who she lives with. She replied, 'I was living with my social worker, Norma, who reminded me so much of Norman by her voice. She changed my life. She took care of me like a daughter would take care of her mother. Then, one day, Albert somehow found Norman. Till today, he never told me how he found Norman. He remains mysterious about it. Norman told me he met Albert in the street. Anyway, that is not important. I am living with Norman now. He should be back soon. Would you like something to drink, dear?' she asked, and I said 'No, I am fine.' Then she added, 'I am blind, but I managed fairly good by myself. Thanks to Norma, she trained me on how to live with my blindness.'

Then, Norman arrived. I could not believe my eyes. I would never recognize Norman unless I hear his voice. Lois said, 'I heard the car. It must be Norman.' I did not say anything. I was stunned, and I did not know how to act or what to say. Imagine, I am in front of a supposed woman, but I suppose to act like he is a man. Lois said, 'Norman, is that you?' He replied, 'Yes, mother dear, it's your son.' 'I am glad you came back in time to see Millie. You remember our young neighbor Millie? Albert had a crush on her.' Norma responded gently, 'Vaguely, mom, it has been a long time and people change with time, you know. How are you, Millie? Have you seen Albert?' I said, 'I am fine, and I have not seen Albert for years. How are you doing?' 'I am doing fine. Thank you,' he spoke. I felt so awkward.

Norman excused himself and let me and his mom talk. Lois told me that it was Albert who found Norman, then he took her from Norma's house and brought him to Norman's."

Jennifer commented, "Poor woman. They played her. Albert does not want his mother to know that Norma and Norman are one and the same person." Millie said, "But guess what? Lois declared that at this point in her life, being an old woman without vision, she could not afford to discriminate. She said that she will die happy, just knowing that her two sons, Albert and Norman, finally got along fine. As for her, she would accept Norman any way he had chosen to live, homo, transgender, whatever."

"'If he chose to become a woman, I can either stop him or I can reject him. I longed all my life for a daughter. I was never blessed with one. I wanted to adopt a girl. My late husband strongly opposed. I did not have much of a voice in that relationship. He claimed that too many children drag people into poverty, and he was afraid of that. He did not want to become poor. That is why he made sure that he left something for his sons, a life insurance policy and certificate deposits (CD.) So, here I am now, no daughter. Before Norman came along, it was a woman who taught me that blindness was not the end for me,' she stated.

'Millie, would you like to see Albert? Hang around a little longer. He's supposed to go to the bank with his brother to sign an inheritance from their father. You know that Norman has been missing for years. He did not even know that his father died. Now that he is back, he is going to the bank to sign some papers with his brother.' Lois wanted me to stay longer, but I had to leave. As I was leaving, Albert arrived in his car, and from the house came out a man in a nice suit. Albert said, 'Wow! Look at you brother, you look sharp. Mom, if you could see how handsome your Norm is.' I didn't say another word. I was genuinely happy to see Albert. We hugged each other and joked around a little bit, and then I left, still confused."

Nancy said, "Norman is most likely a transvestite, not necessarily a transgender. People do that for fun sometimes. Some are even addicted to it. I know a man who is married with children. Every weekend, he dressed up like a woman to go out with his wife. Or it could be that he has to look like a man to claim the money." They all agreed and said that is right because he is identified as a man in the will. Albert was trying to conceal the fact that Norman is transgender. If he is a true transgender, socially, he is a woman.

"That is why Albert was bragging about his brother looking sharp. He did not want his mother to suspect and then connect Norma and Norman. That's all." Everybody agreed. And Genesis inquired,

"How come Lois is destitute and her sons had an inheritance?" Millie answered, "Lois had the house and her share of an inheritance, but it turned out that Roger had some debts that had to be paid. That is how she lost the house and her money. They were not rich people, but Roger had a good job and a little business aside. If you ever owe Internal Revenue Service (IRS), you must pay sooner or later. Internal Revenue Services (IRS) has no compassion. You can commit suicide, the IRS will not care and will collect."

Henrietta, who was listening, said, "I heard you talking about Lois Benton. I knew her husband. He was a nice fellow. Do you know how Norman found his mother?" Millie answered, "No, I didn't want to probe into her personal affairs." Henrietta related, "Norman was transferred from Texas to a New York social security office as a social worker supervisor. He oversees all cases. As he was going through them, he found his mother's file. That is how he knew where his mom was living at the time. So, he rushed to go get her from Viola's boarding home."

Millie said, "O! I see. That makes sense now." Jennifer added, "Albert took Lois from Norma's, turned around the block, and brought her back to the same house, except this time, it is at Norman's house because she is blind." That was funny and they all laughed. Henrietta added, "Even if you would tell Lois that Norman and Norma are the same people and that Norman is a transgender . . ." Millie finished the statement, "She would not believe." Henrietta continued, "She must see to believe, and she does not see. So, you would waste your breath trying to convince her that Norma was Norman all along."

Simone and Nancy announced that they will be leaving in the morning. Simone really wanted to see her father Eli, her half-brother Tyrone, and half-sister Grace.

Back in the male jail, Eli was wondering why he has not heard of his daughter Simone. Tyrone is out of jail and working on Grace's case as an investigator, looking for Lauralee's boyfriend and the father of her children. Errol has a visitor, his wife Marion who brought bad news. Errol's parents are in the hospital affected by the COVID-19. Errol's consent is needed to disconnect them from the artificial respirator (ventilator). Errol is distressed by the news. He is close to his parents and loved them. He does not want to be the one to make that awful decision. His wife reminded him his siblings already agreed to let them go.

Calloway is upset after hearing that it is recommended to wash hands twelve times a day to prevent the coronavirus. He made a sarcastic remark, "Washing my hands twelve times a day! I might as well cut them off. Give me an ax." Another inmate who just arrived was singing loudly, "All is well with my soul, all is well (bis) with my soul," and he inquired, "What time is lunch served?" and continued to sing, "All is well, all is well with my soul . . . How is the food here? I suppose you have three square meals a day. That is better than the street. I am homeless. Prison is better for me. At least, I have a bed, a warm blanket, and away from the coronavirus. I am negative, thanks God. Everybody is positive until proven negative. Stay away from each other. Kiss and handshake are things of the past due to that coronavirus. It sucks."

Errol's friends all gathered around him to console him in his moment of grief. He must let his parents go. The group who used to hang out together has been tested and waiting for the result. If one is positive, he will go into quarantine.

In the meantime, Calloway tried to cheer up Errol by narrating a crippling story. He spoke, "I remember a couple who moved one block away from my home. The husband and the wife were both afflicted by physical disfigurement. The woman's legs were inverted. She walked sideways and one hip was higher than the other. The husband has scoliosis or kyphosis. I am not sure which one he had. They were nice people who got along fine with their neighbors."

CHAPTER 6

"One summer night, something strange happened. A beam of light was noticed hovering over their house and inside the house was lighted with a very bright red light. Neighbors ran over to see if the house was on fire. They called them, no answer. The next day, my mom went over to ask them about the incident. They were not home. After a month of absence, they were reported as missing people. Nine months later, they came back. To everyone's amazement, the two were no longer disfigured, and more surprisingly, they came back with two children, a girl named Rah, and a boy called Little John. Everybody was baffled. The couple claimed that some doctors came to get them in something like an airplane. They operated on them."

"How did they get the children? They could not remember?" Errol said, "Are you kidding?" "No, I am not." Tyler said, "Whatever was on the roof of their house that night is responsible for their abduction. They were abducted by aliens. The police would not do anything. They were afraid, and the authorities did not want to hear about that either. They would silence anyone who is bragging about aliens." "What did the children look like?" Tyler asked. Calloway replied, "They looked human but weird."

Calloway continued, "Their pastor tried to get them (the couple) to talk about their experience. They maintained it was God who came to their house to take them away and treat their physical anomalies.

Nobody believed that was God, even the pastor. However, they were not lying. They really forgot what they went through."

John inquired, "But where did the children come from? Nine months, two children. They were twins I assume?" Calloway said, "No, Rah, the girl, was older than Little John. The girl looked mean and she was quiet. The Little John was loved by everybody because he was a child healer, and Rah was a genius. You will be amazed by what those children did. They were two extraordinary children, out of this world." Errol said, "Don't leave me in suspense. What did they do?" Calloway answered, "After lunch, I will continue."

* * *

"To continue what I was saying earlier, about the children being extraordinary. When Little John was about seven years, it was evident that he was a child healer. When the son of a rich man in town was extremely sick and about to die, everyone in town felt sorry for the family. A boy, six years old, was about to succumb to meningitis, a highly contagious disease. Little John went to see the boy regardless of his parent's objection. The boy's family did not want him to come close to the dying boy, but they could not stop him. He insisted that Michel is not going to die. He simply wants Michel to touch his pinky finger.

The pinky finger, in fact, was strange. There was a tiny red stone on the fingernail, something like a ruby that was part of the nail. So, as he entered the room, Michel who was moribund said, 'Little John, do you come to see me? I am dying, you know.' Little John sweetly replied, 'No, Michel, you are not dying anymore. Here is my pinky. Hold it and squeeze it.' Michel said, 'What is that going to do?' Little John responded, 'My energy will go to you. And now, give me your hand.' Michel extended his arm to him and he gradually stood up. 'Walk now,' Little John said. Effectively, Michel walked out of his room to outside. The parents were stunned. Michel was cured. The news was all over town. Most people in town believed that the parents of Little John were sorcerers."

John said, "They were either aliens or part human, part alien." Tyler said, "I agree. Sorcerers don't do anything good. I don't even believe in them." Jose said, "Calloway, are you talking about the Hill's children? They are not ordinary kids. I know them. Rah, the girl, stay away from Rah. She can be good. She can be evil as well. Let me tell you about Rah, Calloway. You probably recall that incident." "Which one?" Calloway asked. "When a neighbor's dog defecated on the Hill's lawn, the mother asked Rah to pick it up. Rah refused. She said that the dog's owner must come to clean up the dog's excrement. Rah went to the dog's owner, Ann Danley, who refused. Rah said, 'Okay, you do not pick it up, I am not going to pick it up either. It is your dog. You are responsible to clean after your dog. Leaving it on the ground is not good for the environment. Don't be surprised to see it at your table at dinner time.' Mrs. Danley laughed at her, saying, 'What a looney you are, girl! How dare you.'

The ordure remained on the grass. Rah and Little John both refused to clean up after the dog. Finally, the father cleaned it up and disposed of it in the trash that was later picked up by the trash truck. The next day at dinner time, Mrs. Danley herself set up her table and placed the dinner on it. She went to the bathroom to wash her hands, then called her family to eat. As everybody approached, they complained of an offensive smell. The husband said, 'Did the dog poop here?' They looked on the floor and did not see anything. They were shocked to discover a strange plate filled with excrement covered with plastic on the table next to their food. They screamed, 'O, my God! How can this have happened?' Julie, the daughter, threw up. Blanche's husband got upset. Blanche Danley remained silent for a while, then muttered, 'We have sorceress as neighbors. They are responsible.' The husband inquired, 'Who are they you are talking about?'

'The Hills,' she replied, and the husband said, 'How do you know it is them? Why do you pin that on them? They are good neighbors, especially Little John, a very smart boy.' Blanche responded, 'The girl is not nice. In fact, Rah is mean, downright mischievous. She put the poop here.' The husband asked, 'Why would she do that and how can you be so sure? Is there something you are not telling?' The daughter said, 'I agree with dad. How do you know it is Rah? Why are you accusing them of being sorcerers? You despise them. Why mom?' 'I think it is because you do not know them as I do,' Julie said. 'Do you know that Rah is the only one who can explain how to work my arithmetic problems?' 'Stop it, Julie, with this nonsense! Since when a black person is more intelligent than a white? This family suddenly is moving up the social ladder. Right now, they look like they have more money than us. Do you know what that means?' Blanche Danley declared terribly upset.

The husband responded, 'What does it mean, honey, you are going to lose your spot in the social ladder? You worry too much. No wonder why you are getting old so fast. No wrinkle cream does not seem to help. Why don't you ignore meaningless things in life and relax?'"

Omar commented, "I don't understand why Blanche did not talk about the dog incident." Calloway answered, "Because the husband will blame her. She's supposed to clean after her dog. You could be fined for letting an animal defecate on someone's property or even in the street. You should scoop it, put it in a bag, and discard it. Everybody knows that."

Calloway continued with Little John's story, "There was a middle-aged man in town named Frederick who refused to get out of bed. Nobody could understand his ailment. His wife was striving alone with the children while Frederic spent his days and nights in bed. One day, he told his wife that he is going to die. She was genuinely concerned and worried about her husband. She told Little John that Frederic is going to die. Little John said, 'I am going to see him.' When he got there, he said to Frederic, 'Mr. Frederic, you are going to die very soon.' Frederic sat up quickly and said in a humble voice, 'Little John, what an awful thing to say to me I am going to die. I do not want to die. Look at me. I am fine. I eat, drink, sleep well, urinate, and poop every day. Look at me, I can stand and walk. Why would I die?' Little John firmly replied, 'Because you laid down all the times. You don't do anything. Your muscles are getting weaker and weaker. Your blood does not circulate enough. Your brain is getting foggy. You are in the right position for death to take you.' Frederic replied, 'O, no! Little John, I am getting out of bed.' To the wife and his children's astonishment, Frederic got out of bed, changed his clothes, and went for a walk to prove to Little John that he is not dying."

Errol said, "That story sounds so familiar. My cousin was always complaining of being sick. She was a hypochondriac. However, when the doctor told her that she has cancer, she was in denial. She said, 'I have no problem. I don't feel sick at all. The lab probably made a mistake. I have no leukemia. I feel great."

Calloway continued, "Danley fell off his horse. His right leg was injured. He was in pain. He could not get an immediate doctor's appointment. Julie begged Rah and Little John to heal her father. The youngsters agreed to go see Roy Danley. Blanche was enraged. She did not want to see Rah at all. Julie told her that her father is suffering. She knows that Little John can help. Rah and Little John both came to see Roy. They brought with them two small pieces of a plank to make a splint for Danley's leg. Rah has a red stone attached to her pinky fingernail, just like Little John's. She applied it firmly on Danley's forehead and said loudly, 'No more pain.' Shortly after, Danley was fine walking on his leg.

Blanche said, 'Are you aware that the Hills are strangers among us? They are not regular people. Sooner or later, someone will take them to court to make them explain by what power Little John and Rah are performing. Rah designed a plan for a building. Rah made a piano for herself. She can play without ever taking any piano lessons. She corrected her teacher in front of the whole class, and she knows where all the planets are in the galaxy. She guided her parents when it is time to grow crops and that is why they are successful in farming and agriculture. She is not a regular human.' Bruce Danley said, 'You never heard of genius, Blanche.'

'Oh genius, genius my foot! How many black geniuses have you heard of? I also learned that Rah and Little John can manipulate the lottery game, and that is how their parents became rich. Little John took his poor friend (Lucas) from school to buy a lotto ticket. He chose the numbers for Lucas, and guess what? They all come out. That is why you do not see Melanie (Lucas' mother) walking in rags anymore. Instead, she is learning how to drive. Her husband has a brand-new car. Have you heard that Sheila down the street told Rah that her roof is about to collapse? She asked her if she could help her with the roof. Rah said no she could not because she has no ladder. Sheila said to her that her house is a Damocles' sword. Rah who understood the saying was saddened. She asked her, 'Do you have money to buy a lotto ticket?' Sheila said, 'O no, my pastor does not want us to play.' Rah said, 'I am giving you the numbers to play. Only you will know. If you give them out, your loss. If you play, you will win, and you will surely donate to the pastor. He will not refuse it.' Later, that day, Sheila won the jackpot. She did not fix the roof. She moved away. Rah was not an ordinary youth. I am telling you.'

Bruce Hanley said to his wife, 'But why does that bother you? Rah saved me from pain and anguish. I am not on your side for that matter. Who is going to take those nice folks to court? What is the charge, Blanche? I am getting annoyed by your attitude. Something else is eating you. What is it? You should be glad to have such an extraordinary neighbor.' Julie said, 'But what is Damocles' sword?' Bruce replied, 'It means a bad thing, an accident about to happen. In this case, the roof of the house was about to collapse.' 'Oh ooh! I never heard of that saying before,' Julie responded.

'So, tell me, Blanche, are you jealous of those youngsters working wonders?' Blanche said, 'Bruce, have you been hypnotized by Rah and Little John? I cannot stand those people. They look weird. They are freaks.' Bruce replied, 'I would not advise you to call Rah or Little John freaks. They can turn you into a real freak. Blanche, hold your horses, don't confront those people, especially Rah.' 'I will confront her. She should know that she is nothing. I can make her family move away back to the ghetto where they come from. It is a free ride now. Blacks think they can live anywhere because they have some money. I am not leaving because of them. They will have to leave.'

Bruce said, 'Honey, that is a thing of the past, leaving a neighborhood because of blacks. Suppose they were famous people like Michael Jackson, or Jordan, Oprah, Halle, would you move away because of them or make them leave? No, you would want to be their friend instead, right? So, burn the race card.'

Blanche confronted Rah anyway. She waited for her in front of her school. She approached and spoke, 'How did you manage to get into my house to place a plate of ordure on my table? You should have eaten it, you nigger.' Rah said to her in a calm tone, 'From my understanding, nigger is a racial insult, but you are a cretin who cannot even spell the word nigger. Therefore, I have no word for you.

I would rather act. I must teach you a lesson you will never forget. Tonight, as soon you put your head down, you will be compelled to choke yourself. You will bring your right hand to your neck to strangle yourself. Nobody would be able to take that hand off. Scientists call this affliction "alien hand syndrome," your hand acting on its own, meaning independently, out of your control.' Blanche said, 'You are bluffing, you, little scumbag.' Rah laughed and added, 'We will see about that. At last, you will learn to respect an alien nigger.'"

All the auditors commented, "Good. She needed someone to fix her ass."

The storyteller continued, "Later, that day, Blanche cooled off. However, she did not mention her confrontation with Rah to her husband and daughter. At night, when the family was going to bed at the usual time, Blanche was highly anxious and hesitated to go to bed. Her husband asked her why she was not getting in bed. Finally, she laid down. Shortly after, she held her throat tight, and Bruce said, 'Are you okay, Blanche?' She could not answer. Bruce tried to take her right hand off her neck. He could not. He called Julie who came running, calling, 'Mom, put your hand down. Why do you want to choke yourself to death?' Her tongue started to come out and then Julie said, 'Let 's call Rah.' Swiftly, Blanche released her hands and she was gasping, short of breath. Her face turned bluish. She was diaphoretic(sweating). Her eyes came out and she was mumbling, 'Rah, Rah.' Julie asked, 'Did you confront Rah again today, Mom?'

Subsequently, Rah's parents were summoned to court to explain how their children do what they are doing. They wanted them to identify their children since there is no record of their birth in the country. The parents presented themselves to court without a lawyer. One was appointed to them. However, on the day of their trial, Rah and Little John arrived all dressed up ready to defend their parents. It was an amazing moment in the courtroom because it was for the first time two minors were standing to defend their parents. Witnesses, lots of them, were present to support the Hills. Everybody was waiting to hear Rah.

The judge said, 'What makes you think that you can defend your parents?' They replied, 'Because they should not be here. They have done absolutely nothing wrong, Your Honor.' Judge stated, 'I heard of your marvels. How do you acquire all that knowledge?' Rah replied, 'Have you ever summoned a genius to ask him why he is a genius?' The judge raised his head, took his glasses off, and hesitated to answer the question. Finally, he said, 'No, I have not.'

Then, the judge asked the parents to tell them where and when the children were born. Rah said, 'They do not have to answer that. We were born somewhere in the universe. Our origin is no one's concern. It is a free planet, a free world. We don't bother anybody.' The judge said, 'Didn't you put a jinx on Blanche Hanley?' Rah replied, 'You are a man of science, Your Honor. Do you believe in such a thing as jinx? And do you have any proof? Do you know that she called me nigger? Once and for all, what does the word nigger mean to you, white folks?' The judge said, 'I only heard the word. I don't know what it means. I never used it.' Rah uttered, 'Seriously, you never heard of that word?' Then the judge asked, 'Where are you really from?'

'We are from planet Zephirin,' she declared proudly. 'Where is it located?' inquired the judge. 'In outer space, somewhere in the universe, close to the earth.' The judge was flabbergasted. He looked frightened and realized that he was face to face with aliens. Some members of the jury left. The security guards were nowhere to be found. It was chaos in the courtroom. Everybody was looking for the exit. The judge all shaky asked, 'Why did you come here?' Rah and Little John replied, 'How about you? Why did you come?' The judge chuckled and spoke, 'Well, I am from here.' Rah said, 'No, you are not. You, like all other humans, came from outer space. This planet is primarily for animals. There are more animals on earth than people. You realize that, do you not? By the way, Your Honor, why are you really prosecuting us? What is the charge?' At this point, the prosecution called the parents on the stand.

Rah opposed, 'My parents will not be interrogated for no reason. They have not done anything wrong. If you insist, I will have to use my power to stop you. Let my parents go, or all of you in the prosecution team will go blind, till I restore your vision, if I decide to.' The judge shook his head and smiled saying, 'You think you are something else.' 'You do not believe me, so, it's time for a demo,' declared Rah.

Suddenly, the judge and the members of the prosecution team could not see a thing. The judge cried out, 'What is going on here? Why cannot I see? Where is Little John? Rah, are you still here? Let me see.' The others were screaming, 'Please no. Do not do that to us. Restore our vision. You are not guilty. Let us see please.' It was a real brouhaha in the courtroom. The reporters were all over and everybody in the building was running, not even knowing what they were running from. An older man was looking for his hat and cane. Rah saw him. She went and get his hat and cane for him. He regained his vision first. 'Thank you, Rah,' he said, and they shook hands.

The witnesses for the defense were overjoyed. To sum up, everybody regained their vision and the judge said, 'Case closed. You are all dismissed.' People made all kinds of comments. Some said that Rah is a little devil. Their parents, Rosanne and Edward Hill, were free to go home."

Errol enjoyed the tale and thanked Calloway for keeping his mind off the ravage of the coronavirus. He said to him, "Now, I am afraid to go home. It seems that I am safer here. How can that be? Safe in prison, no way. I must go home. My dad and mom were gone. I had no chance to say goodbye. I am so sorry. My drinking problem is responsible."

Calloway said, "You should be released." Errol declared, "*No*, you do not understand. I am a repeated offender. Pray for me, Calloway, I must go to rehab. My wife threatens to divorce me if I do not get sober, and I cannot afford to lose her. She is a good wife, a good mother, she has been so patient with me. She is so easy to live with, never complains, but now, if she said she will divorce me, she means it. Right, Calloway." Calloway said, "Do not let that happen, brother. Go to a meeting fervently. Follow the twelve steps. Do not hang out with alcoholic friends. Once you are sober, forget them. I am an alcoholic too. That is why I am here. I just do not tell my business. You and I must forget the booze to keep our women. Don't weep. There is always a rainbow after the rain. You will make it. Hang there."

Then, Calloway resumed his story when a man who was listening asked, "But what happened to the family after court, Calloway?" He responded, "They continued to live in town, everybody respected them, and they were loved. Little John went to visit an old dying man who was lonely. When Little John saw him, he said, 'I am sorry, sir. There is nothing I can do. I can only keep you company. I cannot get you back to live again because you are old, ninety-seven years old. Are you afraid to die, Mr. Ingle?' The old man replied, 'I am used to life. Where I am going, I don't know. Do you know, my boy, where do you think my spirit will go?' Little John said, 'Are you sorry for the wrong things you did?' Ingle in his weak voice asked, 'Wrong! What did I do wrong, Little John?' Little John said, 'May I sit down, Mr. Ingle?' 'Yes, yes, my son, sit down. Now, tell me, when will I die little John?' asked Ingle anxiously. Little John stated, 'You have one month to live before you die. You are going to stand up and feel good, you will walk again, you will eat your favorite food, and you will reconcile with your brother-in-law.'

'My brother-in-law is my enemy, an implacable enemy,' Ingle said with fear in his voice. Little John explained, 'You should have no grudge against anybody before you die, Mr. Ingle. All your life, you have been a mean person. You were a mean husband, you mistreated your wife, a mean teacher, you beat your students mercilessly, a mean prosecutor, you sent your brother-in-law to prison for a crime he did not commit, and a mean father, you did not show any love to your children; you punished them severely for little things. Your neighbors called you ruthless. Now is the time to be nice. You will have one week before you die to repent and make amend for your wrongdoings.'

'But I am in pain. How come I will walk again and feel good, Little John?' Little John stated, 'I have a theory.' Ingle reacted surprisingly saying, 'Theory! What theory, Little John?' 'Let me explain. I think that all the nerves that carry pain to your brain will die before you. Subsequently, you will have a surge of energy for a short while. For that reason, you will feel no pain. In your sleep, peacefully, you will go without knowing. Death should not be hard. It is like a long sleep. Not as bad as you may think, Mr. Ingle. You are old now. We all must go, so you too will go. I am sorry that you are going.'

Ingle asked, 'How old are you, Little John?' 'I am nine, and my sister Rah is eleven. Goodbye now,' said Little John. Ingle said, 'How do you know so much about me?' He replied, 'I read a lot of books at the library. There is one about you written by your brother-in-law.' And Ingle said, 'Is that so? A book about me? I see. I am definitely an evil man. In that case, I should confess, Little John.' Little John said, 'Not a good idea, Mr. Ingle. Let me put it this way—you must feel sorry and apologize to those people you hurt in the past. That is all. God already knows. Why should you confess? To whom?' Ingle in a shaky voice said, 'Thank you for coming, Little John.' 'Goodbye,' Mr. Ingle John said as he was leaving. 'By the way, what is your first name?' Ingle replied, 'Pericles, Pericles Ingle, like the great Greek statesman.' 'Are you Greek?' inquired Little John. Ingle stated, 'I am half-Greek and half-Irish.'"

CHAPTER 7

"Rah went to see her friend Julie. She would not go inside Julie's house because of Blanche. At once, Julie apologized to Rah on behalf of her mother. She found out that she had called Rah a nigger. She accepted the apology and offered to change Blanche's facial appearance by erasing the wrinkles and tone up her skin with the stone attached to her fingernail (pinky finger). Blanche was ashamed, but her daughter Julie encouraged her to befriend the Hills. In that regard, Rah went to see Blanche to offer her a facial massage. Blanche gladly accepted. She pressed her stoned fingernail on each wrinkle. Instantly, the winkles and all lines disappeared, and her face was flawless, smooth, and firm—no visible sign of aging. So happy, tears came to her eyes. Her husband complimented her on her new looks. Rah was at last accepted by Blanche.

Pericles Ingle's grandchildren organized a party for his ninety-eight birthday. It was on that occasion he got out of bed, cut his birthday cake, and ate his favorite dish, spaghetti with chili and southern homemade cornbread. His brother-in-law Edward Jacobson, eighty-four years old, showed up to everyone's surprise. They have not spoken to each other for thirty years. Rah and Little John were invited. Pericles got out of bed and walked, looked at his backyard and his garden for the last time, said hello to his neighbors, and shook hands with his brother-in-law. Two months later, he died."

Errol asked, "Why was Frederic in bed all the time if he was not sick?" Tyler said, "I know the answer to that. He was depressed. Nobody could understand it. That is depression. He could not get out of bed because he had no energy, no motivation. I know cases like that. In his case, Little John has a lot of energy coming out of him going to him. That is one thing, and the other thing is, no one wants to be told that he or she is dying." "Thank you, Tyler, for explaining. I did not think of it that way. In my point of view, he was just lazy. I don't know better." "Thank you for listening. I hope you did enjoy my story," Calloway said. They all said, "Oh, yes, we enjoy every moment of it."

John said, "I have heard a story about aliens before. A friend of my sister who is a writer was writing a paper, a documentary about aliens and UFOs. He was supposed to submit the document to a university. One night, he was tired of typing; his eyes were also tired. So, he sat down on a recliner in his office to take a little nap before resuming writing. He fell asleep for a while, then he needed to go to the bathroom badly. So, his eyes opened. To his surprise, there were about four entities standing around his desk, going through his documents, reading them. He was so frightened he could not scream. He could not run. He eventually urinated and defecated on himself. He did not have his glasses. He left them on the desk. So, he could not really discern what they were doing. They were going through the document, reading on the computer. He felt like he was glued on the recliner. He could no longer put his needs on hold. He passed flatus loudly. They turned to look at him with dismay, and the beam of light from their eyes came directly into his eyes. He could not see for a few seconds, and then, his vision was restored.

They took his eyeglasses and the laptop as they were leaving. They went through the closed door as shadows. He called the police to report the incident. They came, took fingerprints from his desk, and that was it. The only thing good about the experience was that his vision became perfect. They examined his eyeglasses before taking them. Now, he has 20/20 vision. He has been wearing glasses since adolescence. So, after that story, I believe there is much more to the universe than we previously thought."

Tyrone who was released from jail went on to investigate and inquired about Lauralee's boyfriend. However, he advised Grace to wait for her grandchildren to turn eighteen before making a case against the hospital. Grace agreed with him, then she came to the prison to tell her father. So, Eli was called for a visitor who was Grace. She was happy to say, "Father, I have exciting news. Tyrone did some digging on Lauralee's boyfriend. Guess what?" Eli replied, "What did you find out?" Grace explained, "Do you remember the taxi driver involved in the accident?" Eli said, "Yes, what about him? He was dead, was not he?" Grace shook her head and spoke, "No, father, he is alive living in a nursing rehab center. He is a paraplegic. And there are more surprises, it turns out that he and the father of Melody's children are brothers."

Eli said, "That is a real jam. I think you should leave it alone." Grace said, "Even if I wanted to leave it alone, I would not be able to. By the way, father, Simone called. She was asking for you. I did not tell her that you are in jail without your permission. She is worried about you." Eli said, "Please do not tell. She is a drama queen; will make a big deal about that." Grace replied, "How long do I have to keep lying for you, dad? Is there a real reason for your staying in jail? I am beginning to think that you are following the scammers of the bible." Eli got upset and asked, "Who do you call scammers in the bible?" Grace said, "I am talking about Uncle Laban, tricking Jacob into marrying his two daughters Lea and Rachel, Mother Rebecca, tricking her husband into blessing the wrong son, and finally, brother Jacob, bribing his brother into giving up his birthright. Those actions are unethical and not recommended to a true believer, father." Eli ignored Grace's criticism and asked, "What did Simone say? Is she okay?" Grace answered, "She is fine, and she also agreed that when the girls reached eighteen, they will be told the truth about their biological parents."

Eli was concerned a bit about his daughter Simone. Once again, he questioned Grace about her, "How did she sound when she called you, Grace?" Grace replied, "As usual, why are so worried about her?" Eli said, "Well, I watched on television that some women were arrested for disorderly conduct during a protest by prolife org. I thought I saw someone that looks like my daughter. That is why I am curious." Grace stated, "No, dad, she is not in jail. If she were, she would tell me. Since she did not tell me, I am not going to ask. Honestly, I do not need to know. I have too much on my plate right now. Simone has not heard of her Tyrone either. Tyrone did not answer his phone for weeks. He claimed he was out of town working on a case and he has a new girlfriend. His phone number has been changed. A lot of bullshits. Anyway, he did a good job investigating Lauralee's boyfriend."

Eli asked, "What about the taxi driver?" Grace said, "O, gosh! I am sidetracked. Let me get back to the real subject. The taxi driver was Lauralee's boyfriend. Tyrone tracked him down and he was asking for Lauralee. He was so excited to learn that she is alive, but he swiftly saddened to hear she is a quadriplegic with some mental issues." Eli said, "Did he know about the children, and have you told the children anything about him?" Grace answered, "He believes that the children were raised in foster homes. Tyrone could not tell him the truth without my permission. There is a saying that states, 'The truth will set you free.' Watch out for that. Some truth can place a pair of handcuffs on your wrists and a set of shackles on your ankles." Eli replied, "I do not understand. Why will that truth be harmful, Grace?" Grace responded calmly, "Because he is the father. He has rights, plenty of it." "But remember, he is not the father of the two girls you have now," Eli mentioned. Grace shrugged her shoulders and said, "I don't know anymore. I'd rather not think about the whole situation. That is a real mess."

Eli declared, "In the long run, you will want all of them, your biological ones and your adopted ones. So, it will be the same for Melody. And one more thing, be prepared for the possibility or even the probability that the taxi driver may not be the father. He did not ask for the children. How strange! Unless he did not know that Lauralee has given birth. Be prepared in case their DNA does not match. So, it will not be too much of a shock to you."

Grace said, "No, no. I do not want to think about all of that. Tell me about your time in jail. It seems that you made friends, no fight, that is good. You and other inmates, you made up your group of friends and each of you relates some moments, some experience in your life." Eli said, "O yes, I heard so many interesting stories."

Grace added, "Have you told them about the day Jesus Christ came to town?" Eli smiled and said, "No, not yet. Before I get out, I will tell them that beautiful faith-related story. I have heard of a story about Satan when he came to town." Grace said, "You are kidding, dad." Eli smiled and said, "No, I am not." "What was the town?" asked Grace. "San-Marco," Eli replied. Grace said, "Oh, okay! Well, good to see you today. I will not be back because you will be home soon. Right, father? I love you."

Shortly after Grace left, Tyrone came to visit Eli. He did not want the other inmate to see him talking privately with Eli since they did not know they are related. Eli told Tyrone, "No need to hide. I told them that you are my step-son and that I raised you like my son. I could not hide that any longer." Tyrone said, "Yep! Okay, I see. Did Grace fill you in about Lauralee's boyfriend being alive?" Eli responded, "Yes, she told me. What else did you find about this guy? Do you think he is the father of Lauralee's children?" Tyrone nodded and said, "Yep, he is indeed. He would like to see their pictures, but he does not wish them to see him because he is an invalid, he is not proud of himself. His parents have been trying to locate the children for years to no avail."

Eli demanded, "Did you tell him about them?" Tyrone said, "No, I did not, and I feel sorry for him and for the children." Eli said, "It's a real jam." Tyrone sighed and declared, "No matter when and how the truth comes out, it will cause a heartbreak for the parties involved." Eli anxiously asked, "But what do you think will happen when the truth is out?" Tyrone responded, "It's hard to predict with young people. They will need time to grieve. They will go through the stages of heartbreak. Denial, they will not believe at first. They would want to repeat the test.

Anger, they will be angry at the hospital, nurses, anybody involved in their birth. Bargaining, they will need time to know what to do and how to do it. Acceptance, they will finally accept that it is the truth. They have been raised by the wrong parents. Will they feel sympathy, pity, compassion, not to mention the love for their real parents? I do not know. I cannot predict the outcome of this case. A psychologist would be able to help them adjust. Besides, they will be adults, more able to understand that mistakes happen all the time. That's life."

Eli said, "By the way, your sister was looking for you. Did you get in touch with her? Did you tell her you were in jail?" Tyrone responded, "No, I did not, and you say nothing either. I did not say anything about you. That is my private life. I do not have to tell. If she went to jail, she would not let me know unless I am the only one to bail her out. Simone is very secretive, but she likes to mingle in my business." Eli said, "Well, my lips are sealed." Tyrone asked if Tyler was still there or if he has his court date. Eli said that Jose and Errol went to see the judge, Omar and John are scheduled to go the following weeks, and Tyler is there.

On a Saturday morning, a preacher came to visit the inmates. "My name is brother Hayden Jones. I am not here to preach to you today. I am here to collect all troubling questions related to the bible, what you don't understand, what is kind of confusing to you, and so on. I will take your inquiries, and the chaplain will discuss them with you at his next visit." Tyler said, "I am so glad to hear that. How come Jesus be son of David, when he was and is sinless and David a sinner? Did Jesus need king David to validate him? Joseph was not Jesus' biological father and the Jewish lineage is from the mother. From what I learned, Mary was just like her cousin Elizabeth, both were Levites. I want a clarification on that." Hayden said, "I got you, brother. Next question please." John calmly stated, "For years, I have been trying to make sense of two verses in the bible. Genesis 1 verse 27, God created man, male, and female, he created them to his image. And then in Genesis 2 verse 18, he created man with dirt. This time, he also created a woman. In my humble understanding, I suppose that God created the spirit first which is in his image, and then, later, created the body with dirt. I would like to hear the chaplain's comments on that. Thank you." Hayden said, "Your point is well taken. Next question." Calloway stated, "My name is Joseph Calloway. I have been rather very intrigued by the story of Noah and his younger son Ham. In Genesis 9, verse 24. What is so wrong about a son seeing his father naked, and why did Noah curse his grandson instead of his son, the real offender? Canaan was supposed to be a slave of the other brothers. Did that really happen? From my point of view, the bible is not telling it like it is. I would like to discuss that because I have a lot to say about that." "You have a point, brother, and you will have a chance to discuss the subject with the chaplain. God bless you," said Hayden and he added, "Next question."

"I have a question. I am sorry. Let me present myself first. My name is Edward Lyons. Why would the Lord Jesus in Matthew 16:18 mention the word church, when in Israel at the time, there were synagogues, temples, assemblies, or congregations? The word church in Hebrew was not used at all. I believe it must be a translation error." "Alright, brother, I got you. Anybody else?" asked Hayden. "Yes, my name is Keith. Some people believe that black folks are descents of Ham and therefore, they are dark-skinned and cursed to be slaves. Is there any truth to that, preacher? I know there is not, but I would like to hear what the chaplain has to say." Then, he laughed. "Interesting requests. It seems that is all. So, let us pray brothers," he said. He led them in prayer and was about to leave when one voice said, "On a second thought, I have a question." Hayden asked, "What is your name, brother?" He replied, "Etan." "And what is your question?" Hayden inquired. "I have been troubled by one verse in Malachi 1:3. Did God really tell Malachi that he hated Esau? That is so disturbing to a believer. Malachi was probably drunk. God and the word 'hate' cannot be used together, and besides, why would God reveal such a thing to Malachi who was not a contemporary of Esau?" Hayden just said, "Okay, I understand your trouble with that." Another prisoner declared, "The chaplain will not come because he has no answer to these questions. He doesn't know more than we do." Hayden said, "God has all the answers," and left.

It was time for Tyler to entertain his mates. He asked loudly, "Has any of you been to a bachelor party?" Everybody answered, "Yes." Tyler said, "Good, but the one I am going to tell you about is a little different." Eli quickly asked, "Are you from Capernaum, Tyler?" "No, Eli, I was invited to Bobby Windsor's bachelor party. Do you know him?" Eli said, "I surely do, and I was there for that blinded bachelor party in the night of decision."

Tyler said, "That is why it was called the night of decision. Eli, since you were there, you can help me with little details, if I forget." Eli agreed. "Now, listen guys. Bobby Windsor was a bachelor. However, he had a girlfriend named Nora with whom he had a son called Danny. Everybody knows that Nora and Bobby have been lovers for a long time. But there was one thing people could not understand—why Bobby and Nora do not live together or get married to raise their boy. Well, the reason, there was a vendetta between the two families. Nora's grandfather Matt had killed Bobby's father."

"May I ask how?" somebody said. Eli replied, "Nora's father was a store manager for the Windsors. One day, they got into a heated argument. Later, in the evening, Matt Brunson (Nora's father) got drunk and went to the Windsor's unannounced. Roger Windsor came out to talk to him. He realized that Matt was drunk. He could not even stand.

Roger was about to call his wife to come to get him when Matt pulled his gun and said, 'You deserve to die today, you son of . . .' He drew his pistol and shot Roger in cold blood.

Bobby's two elder sisters, Francesca and Joanna, oversee the family fortune and they never forgot about their father's killer. Therefore, Nora was a forbidden fruit for Bobby, but nothing could stop them from getting together. But still, the two sisters arranged a marriage for Bobby with a much younger girl called Eleni. To Eleni's parents who were working-class folks, they were offered a free apartment in the Windsor's building. They were told that the Windsors have a reserve of gold in Mexico (the land of their mother.) If Eleni marries Bobby, she will become the matriarch of the family when the sisters are gone."

Eli continued, "It was a plan they cooked up with Eleni's family without Bobby and Eleni's knowing." "Really!" exclaimed Tyler, "I did not know the whole story, but I remember the party, which was so entertaining." Eli answered laughing, "Yeah. As a matter of fact, Eleni was in love with Nelson Cunningham. They were college sweethearts." Tyler excitedly said, "Get out! Eleni was already in love with another man and they matched her up with Bobby." John commented, "Where does this story take place? In India or somewhere in the Middle East? Because it does not sound like taking place in America at all. A girl in love with one man and will marry another one, mostly for a reserve of gold. What a lie! Who are those people? Modern-day conquistadores? Continue, Tyler, I want to hear the rest."

"Well, in Capernaum, if a man is twice the age of a young girl and had previous relationships that involve a child or children, if he is still seeing the mother of his child on a regular basis, he must be able to pick the young girl while he is blindfolded. If not, he will marry the mother of his child." Everybody exclaimed, "What? That is unheard of. What has happened to freedom? A man can marry any woman he wants regardless of his age. That is the way it has been since the dawn of day and till now."

Calloway commented, "Do not you hear where it is happening? In Capernaum, the only modern city that has a city gate. How obsolete! The residents are also very conservative there. For instance, two men came to get a license to get married. The clerk said, 'We do not marry two men here in Capernaum.' The couple replied, 'But it is United States.' The clerk sarcastically replied, 'I am sorry, this is not a state and it is not united.'"

Tyler related, "Before the party, the three women, fashionably dressed, arrived. The three were Bobby's love interest: Nora Brunson, the mother of his son, Adele Jackson, an old girlfriend, and Eleni Jones, the potential bride-to-be. The bachelor party would take place after the bride is chosen. In the meantime, families and friends were there, enjoying themselves. Among the families and friends were Nelson and his uncle Laban Cunningham, a rich merchant who would do anything to make his nephew happy. In fact, Nelson was not invited, but his uncle insisted that he be there. So, he came, looking very dashing, ready to pick up the pieces. Their presence caused some anxiety to Eleni's family."

"Sorry to cut you off, but Eleni did not break up with Nelson before that party?" a listener inquired. Eli replied, "Yes, she did, three months before." "Was she in love with Bobby?" "It was not a matter of love. It was a business affair to benefit the sisters. They wanted a woman they can control like they control their two brothers, Bobby, and Stephen who is retarded. They were affluent in Capernaum. They had the means to manipulate other people. Eleni's father worked for them. The family moved from their poor house to live in a much more renovated house in the city," Eli explained.

Tyler said, "I did not know all that because I am not from Capernaum. Thank you, Eli. Anyway, I saw him before he was blindfolded. I wished him luck and added, 'Pick up the right girl, man. You are finally getting hitched. The old days are over, my man!' We laughed and I murmured to his ears, 'Do you have a way to recognize who is who?' He told me the secret is in the perfume. He confided to me that he loves Eleni like a daughter. He loved her since she was a little girl. He knows her very well. She is a lovely young woman. However, Nora is the woman for him. 'I cannot imagine her in the arms of another man and my son with a stepfather. I cannot help those feelings. You know what I mean. A woman who used to talk about you, you are the love of her life, and one day, you become a faded memory of her past. She refers to you as the father of her son. It is hard to swallow, man. That is enough to bring up a deep depression. So much so that you would want to listen to the saddest song with a hope or a pistol in your hand.' I laughed and added, 'A country song would be better with a bottle of tequila to drown yourself in the booze. But listen, man, you are stronger than that, right?' He replied, 'Yeah! but it is a problem, bro!' I continued to comfort him saying, 'Listen, brother, be confident. Nora may have some tricks on her sleeve to win you. Do not underestimate women. They are master brains that can successfully untangle any double knot. Unfortunately, your sisters carry the vendetta against Nora for a little too long. I understand how they feel. Nevertheless, you should not be the one paying the price of that vendetta.' He smiled and spoke, 'Thanks, Ty, I remember the old days. We had fun, didn't we?' 'Yep! We did, and now it is time to settle down. Sooner or later, we must do it. Once again, good luck, my old friend!' And I was thinking about the situation.

If Bobby marries Eleni, he is marrying her to please his sisters and have his share of the inheritance. Then, he would get them off his back. But if, for some reason, Eleni lost, Bobby will be free to marry anyone he chooses to, and Nora will be the winner. So, I said to him, 'I am praying for you, my old friend.' He said, 'Thank you for being here,' and we embraced each other."

CHAPTER 8

"The moment of decision started with a dance. Bobby danced successively with the three ladies in front of everybody. They were dancing without talking. After the dance, people ate and socialized with one another. Eleni's father talked about his family and gave a short history about the Garcia-Windsor family and business.

Francesca talked about the family business and explained how the father, Roger Manuel Windsor, who was an American businessman and entrepreneur died. At this moment, Nora left and then came back later.

Next, Bobby was blindfolded. He was guided to the table where the ladies were sitting anxiously waiting for the process to be over. Bobby walked to Adele first. He danced with her and took her back to her seat, then took Eleni's hand, danced with her, and took her back to her seat. Finally, he took Nora's hand and danced with her holding her close. The music stopped. Bobby pulled the blindfold off. Surprise! It was Nora and that was the moment of truth. Nora was excited. Her friends and family members applauded. She was the chosen one to marry Bobby.

Her son Danny was so happy. He danced and did somersault that captured the attention of the guests, then, he went to his aunt Francesca and spoke, 'Auntie, my dad and my mom are getting married. I am so happy.' Francesca said, 'Congratulations, Danny,

I am happy for you.' Joanna got up from her chair, went to shake hands with Nora, and offered her congratulations.

Francesca was looking everywhere for Eleni who was swiftly taken by Nelson, right after Bobby chose Nora. Laban, Nelson, and Eleni left together. Eleni's parents came to congratulate Nora. As for Bobby, he did not know how to feel. On one hand, he was happy to choose Nora, but on the other hand, he was embarrassed. He felt like he deceived Eleni."

Eli said, "Did you know what really happened? Laban got involved. Here is what he did. According to close friends of Bobby and Nelson, Laban found out what perfume Eleni used to wear. He gave that perfume to Nora as a present and told her that it will bring her luck and that it is the one she should use for the night of decision. She went to Eleni and offered her a brand-new French perfume and told her that it will bring her luck in everything. The perfume was exquisite. She never wore one like that before. So, she wore it for that special occasion. In the end, Nelson got Eleni the love of his life and Bobby got Nora, the woman he absolutely loved, and Danny was one happy little boy with a normal family."

Omar said, "The story sounds a little weird but it is entertaining thus. Mostly, the blindfold part is the fun part." Eli said, "It is an interesting story. However, liberated women would not like it and you know why. They are liberated now. A story like that is considered degrading to women. It makes them feel that a man is so important they would do anything to marry one. Some women would never agree to sit down with other rivals waiting to be chosen. No way, not these days." Tyler said, "In a way, it does make women feel like they are objects to be owned. Well, guys, thanks for listening." One person said, "How was the bachelor party? I suppose after the choice was made, there was a real bachelor party, right?" Tyler responded, "Yeah, we all men had a great time. There were three belly dancers and two strippers. We drank, sang, joked around, and went home. I did not attend the wedding. Eli went for sure." "Did you know Eli then?" he added, and Tyler said, "No."

* * *

John has a visitor, her mother Helen who came to tell him about what her nephew did. A black man was ferociously killed by a white policeman. The black community was enraged. Some protestations turned into a riot. Jamal Wright, John's cousin, was involved in breaking stores and banks. He got arrested and was in jail. Helen Wright said, "Jamal is no nephew of mine anymore." John said, "Why?" Helen replied, "You dare asking why. What black folks are doing in the street right now does not justify their frustrations. They do not represent me as black or the black race in general. Why do they steal? Why do they vandalize, burn down what their community needs? Why break and destroy the very necessities of daily life, such as pharmacies where we get our medicine, banks where we put our money, health clinics, our schools? Will that make the whites respect us? No. We are a bunch of fools. Their actions simply defeat the purpose of the protestations."

John said, "The police had no right to beat up or mistreat a human being like that. There is no excuse for such treatment, Mom." Mother said, "Don't I know that?" John said, "What should people do to express their anger and get justice?" Helen screamed, "An eye for an eye. The mob in the street, instead of breaking things, should seize the officer. He should receive the same treatment without killing. So, he will live to remember what an act of barbarism is. That is what I recommend, make policemen taste their own medicine." John sighed and uttered, "Your prescription is not realistic, Mom. The whites have power. Consequently, they are the true and only racists in the world. We, African-Americans, we are still behind." "Corrections, we are not African Americans. We are American citizens. What part of Africa is yours exactly?" Helen asked. John replied, "We all came from Africa, are we not?" The mother replied, "Our ancestors a long time ago were pulled from Africa to be implanted here. Their bones are scattered around in America. They sweated to bring this country where it is today. There is not one spot in Africa we can call ours. We have no claim in Africa. I am not grateful to Africa. Have you ever heard of a white man identifying himself as European-American or white American? No, he is an American, needless to mention his skin color, because his appearance is self-explanatory unless he is speaking to a blind." "I am a black American." "Why do you have to mention your race? Who asks you? Everybody can see you are black. Isn't it time for us to take possession of what is rightfully ours? This land is our land as much as it is the white men's land. We must be takers, just like them. They came to the new world and took. So, instead of playing around calling ourselves Africans, I am no African. I am an American and that is it, and I am not playing victim either."

"Imagine if the case was reversed—a black man torturing a white man in front of the whole world." Helen commented, "The black world would be on fire." John said, "How can we practice an eye for an eye? They make the laws, laws that are in their favor, Mom."

"I agree with you, son, but still, when it comes to retaliation, blacks have absolutely no tactics, no skills. Walking up and down the street, screaming, and stealing will not bring us respect. The officer was a beast who killed a black man like he would kill a wild beast. He should be treated the same exact manner. As for Jamal, he is a disgrace to the family. I will not bail him out. If his parents were alive, he would not get away with it. Breaking things may mean frustration, but stealing, mmm . . . there is no excuse for that. Now, how about you? When are you getting out of here? Did your wife stop by?"

John said, "Only once. She is still mad at me, Mom." Helen said, "Talk to your attorney to speed up your release. Speaking of your wife, did she tell you about the money her older sister (Clara) was looking for in the house?" "What money?" John asked.

"Your mother-in-law never had a bank account, except for a checking. She kept her money at home. She did not trust banks nor her husband. The couple used to keep their money in a safe at home." John said, "They were lucky they did not get robbed in their lifetime." Helen continued, "After Sylvia died, the children were looking for her savings. The safe had only two hundred dollars. What happened to the money Sylvia got from her husband's life insurance policy with her name as beneficiary? She also sold her condominium apartment. They did not know. She always told her children that she has everything in order, so when she died, there will be no problem and she was not going to die any time soon. How did she know that? Do not ask me, I do not know. She was one complicated woman. Unfortunately, she died suddenly of a heart attack, you remember."

John said, "They had to take loans to pay for her funeral." "Oh yeah, I remember," Helen said.

"Furthermore, Estella was going through a rough time when her daughter Sherri got pregnant unexpectedly and her husband was still in law school. They were facing hardship. So, they came to live with Estella. Every day, Estella and Laura were looking for the money. Laura even went to consult a medium to summon the spirit of their deceased parents (mother and father). She was not successful. The medium called their spirit. They did not respond to the medium.

They lost hope until one day, Laura and Estella decided to have a garage sale. They had a lot of good stuff for sale. It was on a nice summer day. They sold a lot of junks and raised a little cash. Late in the afternoon, as they were packing what was left into boxes, a woman came with a four-year-old girl who wanted a lovely doll that was not yet packed. She sold it to the mother, and the child was so happy to have the doll. Laura looked around and saw a big old teddy bear, picked it up, and was going to give it free to the child. Suddenly, Apollo, the family dog, started barking fiercely at the woman and the child. He chased them away. Laura was in dismay. A dog who was usually friendly, all quiet around her while in the garage then, suddenly turned aggressive. Laura wondered what prompted such a behavior. She could not imagine nor guess. She felt very embarrassed. The woman and the child ran off in fear. Laura did not have the time to apologize for the dog's unpredictable behavior. She scolded the dog for the attack.

Afterward, she placed the puffed animal (teddy bear) on a chair. It has sentimental value. She did not want to discard it in the trash.

Apollo got close to the teddy bear and started to rip it off. Laura got scared and thought for a moment that Apollo is getting mad. She went to the house to tell her sister (Estella). Then, both came out and got the surprise of their life. Money was all over the garage floor. The puffed animal was filled with money, nicely folded inside some clear plastic freezer bags. Many bags filled hundred-dollar bills. The head of the bear contained all the precious jewelry their mother owned, a total value of three hundred thousand dollars (cash and jewelry combined), and a legal document with the names of the beneficiaries, signed and notarized."

John said, "That is mind-boggling! What kind of dog is that?" Helen responded quickly, "A German shepherd." John smiled and uttered, "No, Mom, I know the dog. What I mean is, how does he know about the money?"

Helen related, "The dog was a constant companion to Silvia and her husband till they passed. Laura said that each time she mentioned the money, Apollo always made a noise like crying, trying to say something. She did give any meaning to that. Only now she realized that the dog knew her master's secret. Apollo always wanted to go to the basement or in the garage where her late mother's belongings are. Once there, he usually laid down on Sylvia's recliner. So, you know now that your wife is in possession of her inheritance. Okay, I am leaving now. Please do not tell Nicole I told you the story. She should be the one to tell you. I am not a talkative person, you know."

"Okay, Mom, I got you," John nicely replied. Finally, Helen said, "I am so glad that your mates got along well with each other, but you must get out, Johnny. You know that you should not carry a weapon without a permit. May God bless you." In reply, John said, "You too, Mom, and it was nice to see you. Ask Nicole why she has not visited me." Helen said, "I will intercede on your behalf."

A new prisoner arrived at the Brooklyn Kings County Jail. He hailed, "Hey, you all, my name is Brutus Arcadius. It is my first offense. Indecent exposure. What was I supposed to do if I needed to take a leak urgently? I had just had a beer followed by a cup of black coffee." "Those two have side effects. They make you pee," a prisoner said. "You do not say! I did not know that," Brutus uttered. "Well, now you know, brother." And Eli ironically stated, "Tu quoque mi fili." Omar asked, "What does that mean?" Brutus said, "Eli is teasing me. I am no murderer." Eli added, laughing, "I am here for the same reason you are here (indecent exposure). That is why I said that." They both laughed at the joke. And they explained to the others where the citation came from. This Latin citation is from Julius Caesar dying. Brutus was his adopted son, and he was among the senators assassinating Caesar, so, his last words were "Tu quoque mi fili," meaning, "You, too, my son?"

"What do we do all day, here? Can we play cards, play instruments, have some sorts of entertainment? You know what I mean. Can we read anything? How is the food?" Eli replied, "When you eat, you will see for yourself. As for entertainment, we entertain ourselves. We formed a little clique. We tell jokes, we talk, we discussed the bible, we sing, we discussed our problems, and try to make sense of things in life." Then, Eli busted into tears. The others tried hard to comfort him, but he sounded depressed over an issue. He cried saying, "Oh God, where were you? Do you really let evil prevail? This black brother did not have to die. He begged for his life. Why is the color of my skin like a heavy cross on my back? Wherever the black man goes, adversity follows. But why? Is the Negro's blood different than the others? I should not watch that video. It is alive in my head. He was a Christian with a family. A human laid flat on his stomach; his two arms in chain behind his back. What could he possibly do? How could he fight four armed officers? What a raw crime! I remember him as a little boy. I am his godfather. I was a witness when his parents presented to the temple. Today, watching him being tortured by a savage and no one there to help him, I think he had to be sacrificed. There must be a reason, one that no one knows. The so-called superior race had committed more crimes than any other race. How superior is that?"

Tyler came to him and said, "Calm down now. It is good that you express yourself, you do not keep it all inside, you spell it out. It is a real tragedy, and It is more than just racism. It is also barbarism. He is in peace now. The color of his skin, the shape of his nose, the texture of his hair, and his social-economic rank is no longer an issue. He is free from the world of white folks, white criminals. Where he is at now, there is no racial background or social-economic rank required. Society and social stigmas are non-existent. Some goods will come out of his death. Slowly but surely, things will change for the better. Our brother is a martyr. Let us wait for the table to turn. Nothing is forever, but we need to work harder to make the other races respect us." Everybody agreed. Brutus said, "Start by getting out of jail. Don't fill up the jail cells. Let us be more educated, more proactive in our social duties. Be united, support each other, love your kind. Let us get out of here." Everybody got excited. They wanted to be out of jail. There was a sense of unity between them. Eli was deeply saddened that a black man was arrested and had died in police custody. No, it was more than just a black man. He was his godson, born and raised in Capernaum, US, Eli's hometown.

Errol had left to go to drug and alcohol rehabilitation. Jose was sent to another facility.

At the women correctional, two women, Jennifer and Genesis, are mourning their relatives who succumbed to coronavirus. Jennifer's cousin who arrived from Italy with a ninety-day fiancé visa got married. On the day of the wedding, Gina Altieri started sneezing. What started as an allergy turned into a high fever with a dry cough and diarrhea. The groom soon developed the same symptoms. Within two days, both died.

Genesis's younger sister Samantha who worked for the catering company, the one that served in Gina's wedding, is in critical condition, near death. Half of the guests present at the wedding is either in critical care or already dead. Both Gina's and Jennifer's grandparents died within a week of their illness. Two women were sent into quarantine. Nancy and Simone were released.

Millie received disturbing news. Her son Kendall claimed that his long-gone MIA (missing in action) Vietnam vet father was spotted in Saigon. According to the source, Walter Johnson is one of the Americans enslaved in Saigon. He was seen working on a rice plantation outside of Saigon.

According to the source, he has a memory issue. He does not remember everything about his past. However, he has a family, a Vietnamese wife and children who are also slaves, and they belong to the slave master. Meaning, that if Walt is coming back home, his family will be left behind. Millie stated that her gut feelings always told her that Walt was alive somewhere. The news brought sadness. Walt has been out of her life for over forty years.

She blamed the Vietnam war for her misfortune. Before the war, she was a respectable woman with a nice family. Her husband gone, she was socially demoted. She met another who introduced her to drugs, and she was hooked. Now, even if Walt returned, he would not need her. She is no longer young. She looks tired and old. A part of her would like to see Walt but would not want Walt to see her. In any case, Kendall is determined to go against all odds to rescue his father from slavery in Vietnam.

His first step was to contact the American consulate in Ho Chi Minh city. Then, Interpol will be involved to make the rescue. Millie shares the news with her inmate's friends. She confessed that Walt's absence changed her life. She could not handle life without a man in her life, and that is a weakness. She explained that at one time, she was very spiritual. She was then stronger, but she followed her heart. "Following your emotions is not always a good idea. Do follow your heart not because it can take you where you should not go. My mom taught me to be strong and I was. Do you remember Samson in the bible? He was strong until he followed his heart, the Philistine woman, Delilah. What happened to Samson? Does anybody remember?" Ilda answered, "He lost his strength." Millie said, "That's right. He became a nobody, and today, I am a nobody because I followed my heart. Falling in love with the wrong man, a man strolling in the path of destruction and I tagged along with him. Today, I have nothing—no faith, no God, no love."

Millie is called. She had another visitor, her sister, Kate. "When will you be out of here, Millie? Where is your attorney? You look better here than when you were out. You see, drugs do nothing positive for a person. Drug users do not look good. They claim that drugs made them feel good. I doubt it. You did not look good when you were on drugs every single day. Now, let us gossip. Do you know that a social plague of the past is emerging under a new name? And it is flourishing around the world. Millie, do you know that slavery is back? Would you believe it? I just learned about it, and something else. The state plans to send drug dealers, murderers, back to the south as slaves to work for the government." Millie replied sadly, "That is called forced labor in modern terms." Kate said, "What is the difference? It is also called human trafficking. It is what it is. Still slavery."

Millie said, "What other news do you have?" Kate replied, "Well, did Kendall come to see you or talk to you recently? Have you watched the news at all?" Millie murmured, "Sometimes, I do." Kate said, "You saw the video of the police arresting this dude and suffocating him with his knees. Is not that awful, inhuman? OMG! This officer is maybe a white supremacist. He should have the hood on." Millie was not interested in that subject. She is waiting for Kate to tell her about Walt. However, Kate is cautious about engaging in the subject of Walt because she does not know how to approach her with the information she has. She was thinking, *If her son did not tell her, why should I be the one to spill the beans? If she knows, why does not she tell me what she knows about Walt?*

CHAPTER 9

At last, Millie said to Kate, "Would you believe that Walt is alive and has been a slave in Vietnam for all those years?" Kate quickly responded, "I believe you, I heard the news, but I was afraid to tell you." Millie sobbed and murmured, "Walt is probably coming back, and what or who will I be to his eyes if he remembers me?" Kate said, "You sound so sad and even despaired, Millie. He will be a freeman with no wife, no string attached to anyone." Millie replied, "You are right, slavery has resurfaced. But it's not legal. Once Walt is found by Interpol, his owner will be busted by the police and arrested, and all his slaves will be freed, giving Walt a chance to come back to the state with his new family. Therefore, I will be simply a remnant of his past, an old acquittance, who has nothing in common with his present and his future. We only share a past, and that is not enough to reconnect us and hold a relationship, Kate." Kate replied, "Millie, I am so sorry you feel that way. I would like to hold you and hug you, but you know, social distancing must be observed everywhere and at all times. Speaking of that, this virus is traveling around the world killing people. Only the strong and the lucky ones will survive. You know, Millie, I strongly believe that the government knows more than it lets on. Now, everybody will receive money. That is a lot of money to give away. It is to keep us happy, and not to ask where this virus comes from. Is it from their experimental lab? Is it from a terrorist? Or was it a political plot to hurt another country and accidentally, the world got hurt in the process?" Millie said sadly, "I am not getting any check, Kate. I am a prisoner. While your theory may hold some truth, you must remember, pandemics have happened before. In 1918, the world had seen the Spanish flu that killed millions. This planet is no stranger to plagues. What else is going on in the family? Are all uncles, cousins doing fine?" "Nobody died of that virus," Kate replied smiling. "If somebody has died, it would be the first news I break to you. Nobody dies, but our old friend Grace is going through a hard time. I did not want to fill your head with, you know . . ."

Millie anxiously asked, "What about Grace? Is she sick or something? Is Lauralee okay?" Kate sighed. "First, Grace found out that Lauralee's twins are not her biological children, then a big blast to the family—Lauralee who is bedridden is now pregnant. She has been sexually assaulted. Grace is enraged and distraught by this case. She is suing the nursing home." Millie in shock said, "Get out! It cannot be. What are you telling me? Oh, poor Grace! How much could somebody take? How is her father?" "He is fine, I suppose. I have not seen him for a while. Grace said her father is fine. Furthermore, you should be proud of your son. At least you have someone to lean on. What a fine young man he is. Look how he is interested in his father's case. Why are you not jumping for joy that Walt is alive?" Millie said, "I am happy he is alive, but he has children with another woman. Once a man has children with another woman, things change, you know, no matter how in love you were with that man. The children more than the woman have stolen something from you. The man will never be totally yours. You can fight a woman as a rival and win. But, you cannot fight the children. Therefore, I am in no position to jump for joy. Walt was the love of my life, a swell guy, I remember, but that was in the past. The Vietnam war has swept our love away. I am so uptight. I would like to smoke a cigarette so badly just to relax."

Kate told her, "You are sad. Let me tell you a story to cheer you up. First, do you still believe in spook? Because what I am about to tell you is very unreal and kind of spooky." Millie smiled and asked, "What is it?"

"In a small town called Little River in Haiti, something sensational had happened. It was on a Saturday, open-air market day, early in the morning. A cow sold to a meat merchant named Madame Durant was taken to the slaughterhouse to be butchered. The merchant (Madame Durant) was already at the marketplace waiting for the cow meat to arrive.

Incidentally, there was an evangelical group passing by, singing 'I fly away, oh glory! When I die alleluia by and by' loudly and gloriously, standing at the crossroad near the slaughterhouse. At that moment, the cow was ready to be butchered. But suddenly, it became very agitated, making some strange noise like it was trying to say something. The person in charge of the killing was trying to hold it tight on the slaughtering table. Then abruptly, the cow broke loose, jumped off the table, and ran out of the slaughterhouse. Bystanders, those living nearby, pedestrians, were running after the cow who was screaming 'Moo! Moo! God have mercy, mercy on me!' while fraying its way to the marketplace. It attacked vendors, mostly butchers, and even killed the woman (Madame Durant) who was waiting for its meat as beef to sell. It Injured anyone who was on its path with his horns. In front of the cow was a crowd running away from it by fear, and behind the cow was a crowd following it, by curiosity, to hear what it was saying. It was saying 'God have mercy, mercy, mercy on me. God have mercy, mercy on me!' It ran all the way to the barn where it was from, leaving its droppings on its way. People were in a state of uncontrolled madness—a cow calling God! In the aftermath, many people got injured and some died. Most of the death was related to the stampede. It is reported that the cow had some gold teeth."

Millie laughed, saying, "You are talking about Haiti, the land of supernatural. Superstition rules this country. I believe in spook. I like spooky stories. The best part is a cow spoke and pooped all the way to the barn. Imagine, if this story were true, how frightening would that be to hear a cow talking? I would never eat beef thereafter. Is there anything serious to tell me?"

Kate said, "No. I just wish you could be home." Millie answered, "My lawyer said I will be going to rehab." "That is good news. After rehab, you must leave your neighborhood. Go somewhere else," declared Kate. Millie replied, "Going away will not help. I must have the will to stop. I must hate drugs. Leaving my neighborhood is not the solution. I must be strong enough to say no to drugs because believe it or not, drugs are everywhere." Kate declared, "I agree with you. However, it is always better to change the environment to make it easier for you to build that shrewdness within. If you want to be sober, you do not abide with drug-addicted friends. The temptation will always be there. Where are you going to find the strength to fight it? You need to resist it, sister. We all need a clean break sometimes from the routine of our daily life. That is toxic." Millie finally in a pensive mood stated, "That sounds right though. I will think about it."

Millie added, "What is Grace going to do with Lauralee's baby?" Kate answered, "Tyrone suggested that she should have an abortion because she is disabled and was assaulted. Eli disapproved. You know he is religious. Grace does not know how to proceed. She is in a state of shock. You imagine a person who is completely paralyzed carrying a baby. Who is responsible? It must be a man involved in her care. Nobody knows for sure. The nursing facility must answer. You can never trust men in the matter of sex."

And Millie said, "Is God still around? Sometimes, I wonder, does he really look after us?" Kate replied, "You got to keep the faith. You must believe. Think hard and ask yourself, why are you here? Should you blame God? Does God take care of all little insignificant nitty-gritty things? No, he does not. Because we can do it. He protects us from the big ones we cannot see, we cannot hear. God provides for men to take care of themselves. For instance, you raise a child in a way to take care of himself someday, not for you to look after him forever. That is how I see it. Our parents would not approve. But this is my point of view on God." Millie shook her head and said, "Thanks for coming by. By the way, find out about Walt for me. Be safe now." Kate said, "I will, and you hang in there Millie, the sun will shine again for you."

A week later, the news of twenty Vietnam prisoners of war (POW) rescued from slavery in Vietnam, China, and Japan made a sensational headline that brilliantly exposed modern-day slavery over the world. Some of the veterans did not remember much of their past. Some suffered from post-traumatic stress syndrome. Upon their arrival in Washington, they were received at the Washington DC, VA hospital for psych and medical evaluation.

Among them was Walter Johnson who arrived alone with no wife no children. He did not have any children with his common-law companion, a Vietnamese woman that he was forced to live with since they were both slaves.

While recuperating at the VA center, he was trying hard to remember his son Kendall who initiated the rescue. However, he clearly remembered the girl he used to date in high school. He asked a nurse for a blank sheet of paper to draw. He drew the picture of a girl who was Simone, his first girlfriend. He left her pregnant and ran off with another girl which was Millie. Simone befriended Millie in jail but had not the slightest idea that she was the girl Walt left her for. Walt drew the picture but did not remember the name or the circumstances that separated them.

Walt drew a nice picture to show Kendall of someone that he remembers. His son said calmly, "That is not my mom." He was disappointed and spoke, "No! So, who is that then?" Kendall shook his head. "I don't know, but definitely, it is not my mother." Walt reluctantly asked, "Is she alive?" Kendall responded sadly, "Yeah, she is alive." Walt sighed and spoke, "Does she know about me? How is she?" Kendall grumbled, "She is okay considering she is in jail." "In jail!" exclaimed Walt. "Why is she in jail? She is such a timid, reserved person, what did she do?" Then the dialogue was disrupted by the nurse entering the room. Kendall had to leave. Walt had to go for a battery of tests.

In the meantime, Simone and her son, Benjamin (Benji), were having an interesting conversation. Benji asked her mother, "Is this Walter Johnson and my father being one and the same person?" Simone hesitantly replied, "That is right, he is your father." Benji added, "So, how do you feel? What is going through your mind right now, Mom?" "Nothing, I am sorry he went through that. I would not wish slavery for anyone. But then, seeing him now brings back some sad memories of my adolescence," Simone explained. The son replied, "You must forgive him, Mom. When we are young, we play strong but in fact, we are weak and afraid of taking big responsibility such as having babies. Most guys do not want to get married because of a baby or tie-down for life with a woman at an early age. Maybe he liked you but was not really in love with you."

Simone said, "I know the difference now between like you and not in love with you. I did not know then. And that does not change the facts. It still hurts each time I remember that he did not love me. I thought sleeping with him would make him love me more. I was so wrong! He did not waste time to dump me and never looked back. He was handsome, well-mannered, well-spoken. It was easy for him to get another girlfriend who was younger and prettier than I was. I never met her. My friend told me that she was very pretty and very smart in class. Till today, I never knew who she was. I feared to meet her." Benjamin curiously asked, "Did he marry that girl?" Simone said, "I have no idea. He was out of my life. I did not go on, poking my nose in his business." Benji asked, "Why did you not make him acknowledge me and pay child support? Why did you raise me alone, making me a nobody, a bastard? In fact, I am the victim here. I pay the consequences of your decision. He abandoned you; you made him abandon me. Too much pride does not pay much. I should really be Benjamin Johnson instead of Davenport that is your last name because I have no father. Well, I will meet him in due time. I hope that will not create any hard feelings between us, Mom. If he is single, I will match you up with him. You can count on it."

Simone said, "No, Benji, you would not do such a thing. Let the past go. You do not need a father anymore. Look at you, you are doing fine. You are my joy and my pride. I did not go through shame and humiliation for nothing. You are my trophy, son. He was not there for you back then. Why would he care now? He will think that you have an agenda. You are after something." Benji chuckled and said, "Like what? He is an ex-slave, he has nothing, unless the government gives him back pay for all those years. He will get veteran benefits. I am sure he is one hundred percent service-connected if he was injured in combat. All in all, I heard your concerns, Mom. Do not worry about me. I know what I am doing. You are lonely. If this guy has no wife, I would like to connect you with him. You do not hate the guy. He is an old flame. I would like to see you happy in your later years, and a person from your past would be the best candidate. Won't you agree, Mom?" His mother replied, "You have a good intention. Nevertheless, just because he is from my past does not make him fit for me. Besides, no matter how lonely I am, I still have pride. It is clear I cannot stop you from interviewing him, but I can advise you to be tactful doing so. Do not tell him right on you are his son. You will turn him off and do you know why? There are so many scammers out there. Everyone should be cautious, especially a person with memory lapse. Do not mention me at all. Make him voice what he remembers of his past, and see what I will come up with." Benji nodded yes to his mother and said, "You have a point there. I see what you mean."

Meanwhile, Kendall does not feel comfortable telling his estranged father about his mother, a woman he hardly remembered. Walt was working his memory hard to remember the woman he drew which was Simone. Walt is eager to see Simone Davenport, the young woman in his mind. He did not remember either Emelie Christof or Kendall, his son with Emelie. Emelie disclosed to Kendall that she was not legally married to Walt. They were living together with the prospect of marriage. Then, Walt was drafted and sent to war. Walt was talking about his friends from high school instead of his odyssey in the war and his experience in slavery. Kendall did not have any good news for his mother. Walter did not remember her and the priority at the time was to take Millie out of jail to drug rehab away from New York. He needed money to afford a good rehab for his mother in her hometown of Capernaum, a city that is cleaned from drugs. The hardest thing Kendall ever had to do was telling his father what brought his mother to prison. He was not comfortable talking about the circumstances that led to her arrest.

Amid his thinking, he received a text message from his tennis playmate, Benji Davenport, that said, "Can we meet this weekend? My wife would like to play. Is it okay?" Kendall responded to Benji, "Yes, my wife might want to come along to play as well." Kendall does not talk about his family, especially about his mom, because she is a drug addict. He was not proud of that. So does Benji—no mention of his parents either because he had no father. He was not proud of that either. Anyway, the two young men who are unknowingly closely blood-related will go on playing tennis, keeping their family life private until in due time they will discover their brotherhood.

Brooklyn, New York

Three months later, all the rescued veterans were discharged home. Walt went back to his parents. His mother was still alive and thrilled to see that her son is alive and well. He was greeted by a crowd of relatives: brothers, sisters, nieces, nephews, old friends, etc. It was a joyful moment for them all. It was like a big family reunion. Kendall was away, taking care of placing his mother in a very distinguished Christian rehab center called the Good Shepherd. There, Millie will remain for six months. Her boyfriend Keith, out of prison on parole, would live in a halfway house in his village of Emmaus, Pa.

Benji had all the information about the gathering in Brooklyn. He went and brought him a present. In a greeting card, he inserted a picture of his mother taken with Walt in high school. Walt's mother, Carmella, spotted him and made a stunning remark. She called him and said, "You look exactly like my husband when I met him." Then a son Oscar came and said, "Wait a minute, who are you? Am I seeing the ghost of my father or what? Tell us who you are. You look totally like my old man when he was young and strong." Benji was speechless. They all came around him like he was important. Carmella called Walt and spoke, "It is either he is your son or my late husband's son with another woman. Which one is it?" Everybody laughed. Walt in dismay said, "You just handed a card and a present, right?" Benji responded with a smile, "Yes, Mr. Johnson." And Walt said, "Thank you very much. I appreciate that. I am going to open it soon." Then, a sister, Sophia, arrived asking, "Has anybody ever heard of Emilie?" Sadly, the crowd said "No." "And how about her son?" Everybody said "No."

It was time for the guests to eat and socialize with each other. At that very moment, a reporter came to interview Walt. He refused stating that the moment was not proper. He was getting reacquainted with some old friends and family members. He will allow the interview another time. He went to the house and came back with a drawing and asked his guest if they recognized this young woman of his past. Benji was astounded. It is his mom. He quietly withdrew from the gathering. He left with a sense of satisfaction, a feeling of belonging. All those folks are his relatives. They were so warm and kind to him, greeting him like he was a prince. He looks exactly like his grandfather, giving him a sense of pride. As he drove away, he remembers his mother's words, "Let it play out. Do not push." Benji did not identify himself as a son. He was pleased with what he did without his mother's knowledge, taking a picture, replicating it, and giving one to Walt. He will find his answer after looking at an old photograph that captured the romance between him and a young girl (Simone).

Shortly after, he exited from the party. Walt opened his present. It was a pen with his initials. He looked at it and liked it. He smiled, opened the card, read what it said, and saw that it's signed by Benji Davenport. Lastly, he took the picture and looked at it, then went to compare it with the drawing. He sighed and whispered, "But this is the same person. The man who handed me the card is Benjamin Davenport. Davenport, Davenport, where did I hear that last name? And who is that girl with me here in the picture? I need a name. A name is important. Without a name, I cannot investigate that woman. I remember her face clearly, but what went on between us? Who is Kendall's mother? And why does this man look like my father? Am I his father and the woman in the picture his mother? Did I have a child I do not know about? Did I abandon a pregnant girl? Oh, God! Maybe I did. Benjamin left without saying goodbye. I must dig further for the truth. Benjamin and Kendall are the keys to my past."

He told his brother Oscar about the picture that came with the card. Oscar said to him, "First thing to do is to go to your high school yearbook and compare the photos. You will find a name for your drawing. My theory is you probably got some girl pregnant. She never told you, or she did tell you, then you dumped her like we used to do in the old days, run away from responsibilities. My dad would have been hard on you. So, you were scared and overwhelmed and kept it a secret. Benjamin identified himself as a Vietnam vet sympathizer. He is probably or most likely your son with the woman in the picture. You do not need an investigator, man. You can pay me right now for solving the puzzle. Benji is your son with the woman in your drawing, and Kendall is your son with Emilie, your living girlfriend, the one you were going to marry at Capernaum on collective wedding days."

Walt said, "Well, things are more complicated than I anticipated. Two women, two sons. I have a lot to think about. I am not rushing to regain my memory back." "Why?" Oscar inquired. Walt said, "The past might drive me insane." Oscar grinned and said, "How coward of you. What is so damaging about your past that you do not want to face it? Are you serious, brother?"

Lyle and Rodney, two high school buddies, arrived with a pack of beer and a bucket of fried chickens. They yelled at Walt, "Hey man, what's up? If you do not forget us, identify us please." Walt was excited to see them and he called them by their first name. He could not remember their last name. As the gathering came to an end, Walt's mother was looking for Benjamin. She wanted to know who he really was since no close member of the family seems to know who he was.

CHAPTER 10

The next day, Walt and his brothers, Frank and Oscar, went to the basement to look for a clue about the unknown woman in the picture. A high school yearbook was found. Walt was able to find a match for the drawing and the photograph—Simone Davenport. More importantly, he found the last letter from Simone that reads, "Tis the last time you would hear from me. I soiled myself by sleeping with you. Now that I am pregnant, you do not share my hours of troubles. Instead, you have found comfort in the arms of another girl. I never meant anything to you. I will have an abortion because I do not want any part of you, just like you do not want any part of me. Do not look for me, do not pity me. I will get back on my feet someday. Your name is not easy to remember but I will never forgive you. Goodbye, Walt. Signed by Simone Davenport."

His brothers read the letter and it was clear that Simone had changed her mind about the abortion and had the baby who is Benji.

Walt started to remember the atmosphere of the high school, the friends he had, and mostly a group of girls that was extremely popular (a clique) then. They were matchmakers and matchbreakers. Simone was part of the group. It was through them he had met Simone, and they were the ones who reported to Simone that Walt was seeing another girl. In another word, the clique was responsible for the makeup and breakup of that relationship.

Walt explained to his brothers that Emilie was just a friend. When he found out about the pregnancy, he was troubled. He did not know what to do. Emily listened to his troubles. He then found solace in that friendship. Emilie was more like a sympathetic shoulder to cry on. It was only later when Simone did not return to school he got involved with Emilie. Even then, he was still in love with Simone. Walt's memory was revived when his friend Lyle started to mimic one of the girl's high-pitched voice, saying, "Walt, my friend thinks you are very charming, your smile worth a million bucks." Walt laughed and remembered Angie, Simone's friend. Then, he replied, "Who is your friend?" She stated, "Simone Davenport, the preacher's daughter. You know who I am talking about, Sunday school teacher, Eli Davenport." Walt ironically said, "Alleluia, praise the Lord!" Angie said, "I can see that you are a loner, walking around campus with your hands in your pocket; shy, so shy, you do not even say hi to girls. What is the matter with you? I am throwing a birthday party for my sister on Saturday. Would you come?" Walt remembered saying, "If Simone will be there, I will come." Angie said, "She will be, but do not mention what I told you, please. It was not meant for you to know. It was, you know, girls' talk about boys. She would not want you to hear that coming from her. She is kind of shy." Walt replied, "And why did you tell me then? What is the big idea? Do you have an agenda?" Angie smiled and responded. "To hook you up with her. You are a lonely soul on campus, and she is a lovely but lonely girl. Her mother just passed. She needs a friend to comfort her. You fit the bill. You are a debonair." "Thank you for inviting me. I am truly flattered. I will definitely be there," Walt said nicely, and he was elated to tell his friends that his memory is coming back gradually. He credited that to the yearbook, the pictures, and going over the high school memories with his friends. All that was helpful.

Benji told his mother about the family gathering and she asked him, "How did you identify yourself?" Benji replied, "As a Vietnam vet sympathizer and a neighbor." He also told her that Walt drew a nice picture of her. She is the woman he remembered. He simply could not attach a name to the picture. Benji pointed out, "Walt's memory is blurry. He can only remember bits of events, recognize some friends, and forget some. He said truly little about his years in slavery. He was first missing in action, then was found and became a prisoner of war. He and a few other GIs escaped from prison and found refuge on a small island. Finally, they were rescued by Chinese who sold them to the Vietnamese." Simone inquired, "What caused the memory lapse?" Benji answered, "From what I heard from the news, a plane crash resulting in head injury is most likely the cause of the memory hole." Simone was happy to hear that Walt drew her picture and she is the one he remembered. Benji observed the change in his mom's attitude toward Walt. She did not want to hear much about him, but now, she became curious. She wants to know more about him. Simone inquired, "Who really rescued him from slavery?" Benji answered, "He was a Jamaican agronomist sent to Vietnam by his government to observe some techniques in agriculture, especially in rice growing. He saw a black man maneuvering a sophisticated machine. He talked to him and realized something was wrong when he asked to show him around. Walt answered that he could not and showed him his leg. He had a device on his leg that will not allow him to escape. He did not want to speak much. He was very apprehensive. The boss talked to him harshly in front of him. He bowed and walked backward in the presence of the boss. The agronomist felt unworthy to see a black man being mistreated and humiliated. He swiftly recognized that Walt was not a free man. He contacted the American consulate and reported his suspicion. As a result, he was advised by the consulate to leave Saigon immediately. Otherwise, he would be in great danger. Consequently, Interpol made an arrest, and a group of people including some twenty American veteran men and women were rescued from servitude in Vietnam."

Kendall returned from Capernaum and left his mother at the rehab mourning her separation with her boyfriend Keith.

Benji and Kendall met for tennis. Neither one talked about Walt. Kendall avoided the conversation when Benji's wife mentioned Walt Johnson. She is also in the dark. Her husband did not involve her in the case. She said, "How come people are still in slavery? I think it is fake news. There is no such thing as slavery now. How could that be?" There was a silence following her remark. They kept on playing.

Meanwhile, Walt's relatives were helping him back to normal daily life. For instance, his niece, Debby, had found Benji on social media. He is a social worker employed by Saint Andrew medical center. His mother Simone is single, never married, and worked as a physical therapy assistant at Saint Andrew as well. Benji is a father of two. She also found Kendall who is a pharmacist working also at Saint Andrew and a father of one. With that information, Walter is ready to track down the rest of his family including Simone.

In the city of Capernaum, Emily has been in rehab for three months. There, she has met an old friend from college, Robert Vaughn, who is a substance abuse counselor. They were happy to see each other after thirty years. Emily was delighted to see a familiar face and hopeful. Robert was a widower with three adult children. Love is on the air. The two were once very fond of each other. The lovers of the good old days have found their way back to each other. She had known Robert long before Walt. Robert's parents had moved away. So, they lost each other. With Robert Vaughn back, Emily had a new outlook on life and a better future on the horizon.

However, Walt remembered Emily and felt that he must, some way, somehow, meet her. He could not proceed to settle down yet with another woman until he meets Emily in person. He was still emotionally attached to her. He strongly believed that meeting her will bring him emotional closure on their past lives. He would like to see Emily doing well. Only then, he will feel free to settle with another woman. Remembering Emily and his son Kendall does not make the decision easy for him. Walt felt kind of torn between the two women.

Simone is relieved to hear that Walt remembered her. However, she is not convinced that love is the reason. She is cautious not to read too much into that reaction. The question she is asking is, "Did Walt remember her because he disappointed her in the past? Could it be a feeling of guilt that made him remember her?" Only Simone's letter to Walt will clarify that unfortunate misunderstanding of the yesteryears.

Kendall has disturbing news for his mother: Keith who promised to return to her once he is free of all charges converted to Islam and took a Muslim wife as well. When he broke the news to her, her response was unexpected, "I am glad he has found religion and a wife. May God bless them. Now that he is a new breed, he would have no need for weed." Kendall said, "Mom, are you okay? It does not bother you. Keith got married." She replied, "I will get married someday. Have you heard of your father? Did he get his memory back? Did he remember me? Anyway, say hello to him for me. I met an old pal, Robert Vaughn. He is single and available. I liked him then, and I still do now. Do not worry about me, son. I will come out of my drug problems victorious." Kendall said, "If you mean it, you will, Mom."

Oscar, Walt's younger brother, told him to put a relationship on hold for now. He must find his way back to normal life, what benefits are out there for him, and how he is going to spend the rest of his life. Walt seemed obsessed with looking for his woman in life before the war. His older sister Arlene came to see him and invited him to go out. Walt asked her, "Where are we going exactly?" She replied, "To the store. Walk around to refresh your memory a little bit. You remember Flatbush and Nostrand avenues, right? It has been a long time since you have seen this vicinity." Walter said, "Sounds good." He got dressed and ready to go. Arlene said, "You need a mask, brother. This is the year of the virus, the year of the mask." "Why do I have to wear a mask? Inside the bus, I understand, but why in the street? Is that a new style or what?" Walt inquired. Arlene answered, "Walt, listen, tis virus is a killer. Suppose an infected person sneezed or coughed, and then, you come to pass while the droplets of this virus are still floating in the air. You will breathe them. And that is enough to take you to the ground or to the incinerator. Do you understand now? The mask is not a fashion statement but a lifesaving one. However, if you are walking alone in a park where there are no other people, that is fine, no mask required. But where we are going is a commercial quarter, Flatbush/ Nostrand junction. Get a scarf and use it as a mask." Walt agreed and went out with his sister.

Kendall had her mother and Walt speak over the phone. Their meeting was bittersweet. They shed tears since their relationship was really coming to an end. Emilie has finally moved on with Robert. Walt knew Robert Vaughn from college. On one hand, he is happy that Emilie had found the help she needed, and she is content. On the other hand, he felt that he is out of her life. And that took him back to an awful memory, the day he received a letter from Simone delivered by Minerva, a friend from the clique. He remembered her words with an attitude, "Here, this is for you, she does not love you anymore. You are out, that is all, bye Walt."

He remembered how he felt at that moment, broken apart and alone. His old friend Matt told him, "You made a big mistake, man, and let me give you a piece of advice in the matter of girls. Do not ever talk about your girlfriend, your wife, with another girl or another woman. Just you would not like your girlfriend to talk about you with another guy. Go look for Simone to work things out with her. If she decided to have an abortion, be with her, support her." It was not as easy as it sounded. Not only was it too late, but Walt was fearful of Simone's father and her big brother Tyrone who was so intimidating. To secretly take Simone to an abortion clinic was too daring for him. He was afraid of taking such a big and dangerous responsibility. So, when Simone did not show up for school, he felt relieved of a burden, but at the same time, deeply guilty.

As of now, he knows where thing stands with Emilie. Therefore, he can hopefully project a future with Simone if she accords him another chance.

Benji met with Walt who explained everything to him. He gave him a copy of the letter Simone had sent to her forty years ago. Simone meditated on the letter and reflected on the past. She remembers her friends, thinking about where they are. She knows that Minerva died in a car accident but has no idea of the others. She felt that she should apologize to Walt and help him get back on his feet. After all, he is Benji's father.

Arlene asked Walt, "Why are you so reluctant to tell us about your years in slavery? I am curious. What did they make you do?" Walter replied, "If I were a woman, I would have a lot to tell you because women are more mistreated than men. They are forced to work as a prostitute or some men concubine. It is sex slavery for them. As for me, if I claim that I was mistreated, I will consider that an offense to my ancestors who really were slaves. I was in forced labor. I was often humiliated. I was forced to have a woman that I did not like at all. I had a tracking device on my body. I could not go anywhere, I had no contact, I could not watch television, or use a phone. I was fed three times a day. I had my own portion of food. However, I could also eat leftovers of Vietnamese cuisine. I had a piece of land. I could grow my own crops. So, that is nothing compared to what my ancestors went through in slavery.

I am totally grateful to this smart Jamaican man who pulled me out of that life. It is unfortunate. I did not have a chance to see him again to express my gratitude. His name is Richard Owens. What a man! He understood my body language. I would never trust anyone saying that I am a slave because if the master would find out, I would be beaten to death. Owens understood that something was not right with me. He then became a whistleblower."

Arlene said, "You suffered then, morally and emotionally. Did you keep your faith all these years?"

Walt said, "One thing that kept me going is a story my father told me about a slave in Haiti. His name was Homer. This story gave me strength. I know one day, deliverance will arrive for me, one way or another. Two identical twin brothers arrived on the island of Saint Domingue (Haiti) as slaves, captured in Congo. They were two mighty hunters, tall and very athletic. They could read and write and were both medicine men. After three long months of misery on a slave ship, they arrived in Saint Domingue. The two brothers who were always together were separated for the first time in their life. One was sent to the south and the other to Artibonite valley.

Hector was sold to a colon named Edmond Theo. He was put on the field to work. Later, he was transferred to the city to be more of a butler. When the master was away, he was there to protect the family. In this household, he met a beautiful young female slave called Meramee. Meramee and the other slaves showed him around. He did not speak the language of the Creoles. However, Meramee was the only slave who understood his dialect because her mother is from Congo. Meramee is a mulatto. Her father was Edmond Theo, the master. She remained in slavery because she was too dark, her hair too nappy. Edmond's wife said no, that girl is not her husband's daughter. Her father must be a mulatto, not a white man. She did not want her to be a sister to her children. Therefore, Meramee was not acknowledged by Theo. So, she was a slave like the others and her mother was not freed either. Instead, Naira her mother was sent to another family as a punishment for practicing voodoo in the master's house. Hector, who was grieving for his twin brother, finally found some consolation in Meramee who was lonely without her mother around. Ultimately, both fell in each other's arms. Together, they have two children.

One day, the mistress declared that she is selling Meramee. The master said no she is not going anywhere. The woman said she must go. The husband insisted asking why. The wife revealed that her nephew who just arrived from France thinks that he is in love with Meramee. So, to please his wife, he decided to send Meramee far away and that was a blow to Hector who is attached to his companion and children. Meramee would leave with the children. Hector tried to supplicate on behalf of his companion. He was knocked down and beaten for talking too harshly to the master.

Two days later, he died of his head injuries. Meramee and the other slaves buried him. All the domestic slaves in the area mourned him for he was such a nice man. Meramee was not sent away. The father, for the first time, showed some compassion. He requested another male slave to replace Hector.

In the south, Homer learned from his master that he will be going to Artibonite Valley. He was sold to another colon. He was escorted by a slave driver to make the journey to Artibonite. Homer would never imagine that his arrival in Little River would cause such hysteria. When he arrived, the master was away. The first slave who saw him fainted. Another one came to see what was wrong with him looked at Homer and he, too, fell unconscious. However, Meramee came out to greet him and was simply dismayed to see that he was Homer, the brother that Hector was telling about, coming to replace him. Homer greeted her and asked, 'Do you speak Kikongo?' Meramee said, 'Yes.' Then, he asked, 'Do you know my twin brother Hector? I believe he is in this town. That is the only reason I am happy to be sent here.' Meramee did not know how to tell the truth without hurting him. He was so happy, hoping to see his brother.

Unfortunately, the mistress of the house came out to inspect the slaves. She looked at him and fell flat on the ground, unconscious. Homer is asking what is going on—why people are falling unconscious. He wanted to revive the lady of the house, but Meramee said, 'No, let her on the ground to die. I can finish her up myself.'

Simultaneously, Hector's three lads came out and saw Homer. They cried, 'You must be Uncle Homer!' They surrounded him in a big embrace, and they wept saying, 'Our father is dead. Are you our father now?' He was confused. He smiled and said, 'What are they saying?' Meramee busted into tears and told him the sad truth. 'Hector has died two months ago.' He said sternly, 'My brother died of what?' Meramee said, 'He died after he was beaten savagely. He hit his head against the ground.' 'I see,' he responded, and quickly, he went out to revive the slaves who passed out. Then, he came back to hear more of his brother's passing.

The mistress was brought to bed by the slaves. Her children tried to revive her. They could not, but Homer did go to her and revive her although Meramee told him to let her die. He said to Meramee, 'Let her live. I have a bigger plan. Death is not always a weapon of choice for revenge. We all will eventually die. I will avenge my brother, my way, in my time, and there will be no proof, and more importantly, nobody to condemn and kill savagely for it. So, let her live.'

'Are you religious?' He asked, 'Why do you ask me that?' Meramee replied timidly since she was not sure what response would please him. Homer said, 'Be aware that religion is white men's magic to suppress other races. Every law, every commitment, was written and given to others by white men. Even a black magic book is written by a white man. All prophets were all whites. Or so, they say. Do not listen to a priest, pastor, minister, whatever they call themselves. They are all defiled, all crooks. You must be intelligent. Do not listen. Do not bend your head down for them to pray for you. That is so stupid. They do not like you. Why would they pray for you? They simply want you to serve them forever.' 'But Homer, what is your plan? You can get killed like your brother,' Meramee stated. 'My brother became a Christian. He swallowed everything. He was not like that, in Africa. We do not turn the other cheek to no one. We were not afraid of nobody, the law, yes. We respect the law but afraid of another being, no. Christianity taught him to love his enemy, his oppressors. What a moral exploitation! Love your enemies, why? They do not understand love. Will they love you back? Jesus was not wrong. He had to say that because he only knows love and it would be wrong for him to say "hate your enemies." Otherwise, he would not be a charismatic figure to worship today. But I cannot follow him. His teaching is not for me. I am a slave, a man in bondage who is considered less than an animal. How can I love my oppressors? Do you realize that is not possible for a human to do? To love those French bastards. Do you sincerely believe that religion is in your favor and that one day, you and the masters will be with God?'

Meramee replied, 'God means goodness.' Homer replied, 'Are your masters good to you?' Meramee said, 'Why don't you believe in God? One day, he will deliver us. God gives us strength to endure.' Homer screamed, 'Strength to endure what other human beings are doing to you? O, I do believe in the god of the universe, but not the way you do. The strength you need is to fight, not to endure. Besides, the God of the gods has nothing to do with me. Slavery is a man-made practice. God has nothing to do with it. We must fight our battles and keep God out of it. We made our bed. We sleep on it. Slavery is everywhere for anybody who is unlucky to fall into it, like me and my brother. If I would get the chance to enslave those masters, I would do so, and mistreat them just like they do to me.'

Meramee said, 'Why didn't you free yourself instead of coming here?' Homer said, 'I wanted to be free with my twin brother. I could never really be free with him still in bondage. In that respect, I am fully responsible for my life on earth, more especially, my freedom. God will not come down to deliver me from anything. He had provided for mankind to take care of themselves when he bestowed a part of him to us, intelligence, although the common belief is that blacks from Africa are all dumb, they do not read or write, nothing good ever came from Africa, all Africans are poor, black is a cursed race, and this is a white men's world. But little do they know about Africa and Africans. Why do you think I am here? My father made a deal with an Islamic merchant. He was faulty on the deal. He promised gold and diamond in exchange for guns, but he could not deliver the diamond. So, the merchant took me and my brother in exchange for the diamond. We went from Congo to Saudi Arabia. There, we learned Arabic and other skills while in bondage. Now, you know the circumstances that brought me and Hector to the new world. As for the masters, I will destroy them somehow after I get everything that I want. I heard you say that God is with you every minute, every hour, in your misery. Is that so? I found that testimony coming from you, a powerless slave, very presumptuous and even disturbing.' Meramee said, 'Do not kill my father or my brothers, please.' Homer said, 'Why would I kill your father and brothers?' Meramee said, 'He is the master. Master Theo is my father. His wife, Amelie, stands against him acknowledging me.' Homer said, 'Oh, I see, you are not totally black. Thanks for telling me. You are more of a foe than a friend, so, we can no longer be allies. By the way, why are you not acknowledged?' Meramee explained, 'My mother was sold once to a colored man, a mulatto named Pierre Pascal. She was caught having sex with him by his wife. She beat my mother up and then sold her to Theo. When she came here, she engaged in a sexual relationship with Theo and then I was born. So, Amelie said that I am not a mulatto, I am a griffe.' Homer asked, 'Griffe! What is that?' Meramee replied, 'The daughter of a black and a mulatto. People talk about me. They say that I look like Mr. Pierre Pascal, the mulatto, and there is no way I could be Theo's daughter. I am way too dark, my hair too nappy, but Mr. Pascal likes me, I suppose. He gave me clothes and foods when I needed it but secretly. His wife hates my mother, and Amelie hates her too. That is my story.' Homer sighed with compassion and said, 'So, it seems that in this country, it is not gold or diamond that rules. It is the skin color.' Meramee added, 'A female slave body is dog meat. Every male in a household can sexually abuse you on a daily basis, and the wife would beat you up or even have you killed if she caught you in the act.' Homer responded, 'And your religion teaches you to love them anyway. Therefore, you are a powerless woman. Remember, you are a woman first before you are a slave. You must learn to fight back if you dream to be free.'"

Walt said, "To make the long story short . . ." And his sister replied, "No, no, I do not want a short version. Tell me the whole story. I am listening attentively. What happened to Meramee? I am interested in Meramee." Walt continued, "She was sold to Theo's brother-in-law and eventually had a child for Philippe Saint-Felix, the son of her new master, Amelie's nephew. Consequently, she was set free since she became the mistress of a white man.

Homer and Meramee went different ways because they were in a different course in Saint Domingue."

Arlene said, "I can understand that she loved her father even though he rejected her. Normally, Homer could no longer trust and confide in her because he was not sure where she really stands." Walt continued, "One day, Homer went to the woods and came back with some fruits. Among them was a wild fruit mostly found in Congo and Madagascar. Nobody in Saint Domingue knew what kind of fruit it was, but it was a eureka moment for Homer. He had found the weapon that will lead him to freedom." Arlene asked, "What was it, Walt, poison?" "No, not exactly. In terms of avenging his brother, he promised to avenge his brother but had no idea how he was going to do it. But when his master who was away was coming back home, the wife just delegated him to go pick him up on a chariot. It was then that Homer made a plan to frighten him by wearing his brother's garment with his hat and a red scarf around his neck. The master had no clue that the new slave is a twin brother of the one that he killed. So, you get the picture when he saw Homer. He cried, 'Is that Hector? But he is dead. Go away. You are a ghost.' He fell off on the ground and hit his head against the concrete just like Hector did. He died instantly in front of his friends who were also frightened and ran away. Homer picked the body up, placed it on the chariot, and rode back home. Most slaves believed that Homer was Hector in a zombie state. For Homer, the death of Theo satisfied his desire to take revenge for the death of his brother whereas Meramee mourned the passing of her estranged father.

Homer gloated over his death. He had one settler down and planned to bring more down and get all slaves free. Amelie his wife was inconsolable and on the evening of the wake, Homer was the servant. He made a tropical fruit cocktail juice mixed with wine and the wild fruit that he discovered. All neighbors who came drank the cocktail juice, and then all became high, unusually friendly with the slaves because, in their visual hallucinations, they saw only white people around them. They experienced all kinds of hallucinations. They danced with no music playing. Some were having sex in front of each other. They danced with the slaves, calling them 'my son, my grandson.' Amelie wanted to make love to Homer calling him mon cheri (my darling). They all went home in ecstasy. The next day, a neighbor, Charles Dupre, came asking for the cocktail juice that made him sexually potent and euphoric.

After the funeral, friends and neighbors came to see Homer and asked him to tell them what kind of juice it was. Homer acted like he did not understand French. He kept on laughing and saying, 'No French.' Amid this occasion, Homer had discovered a box of legal forms in his dead master's office. They were freedom papers. Homer filled them out, and after serving juice to Amelia and making love to her, he made her sign them all while she was high-spirited.

After Theo was laid to rest, Amelia handed freedom papers to all the slaves in her household. Some of them were happy to leave immediately while some others remained in the house which they considered their homestead. Homer and his nephews decided to stay, not because they had no place to go but because Homer envisioned that the mansion and everything in it will be his when the mistress died or left the island since Theo's two sons will be going to France to pursue their education and would not return.

Homer made a business of selling the cocktail juice to white folks who became addicted. Therefore, a class of drug addicts was born in Little River. There were the masters who could not function without a 'fix.' The slaves called them 'les dejoués' or 'the foiled.' As for Homer, he became a rich freedman whose first duty was to place his brother Hector's remains in a decent casket that he constructed himself, and then, he buried him in the freedmen cemetery. The slaves of the neighborhood, Meramee and her sons, Meramee 's mother, and Naira all gathered together. In a simple Congolese-style burial ceremony, Homer mourned over his beloved twin brother and buried his remains hoping someday, he will bring his bones back to his native Kongo.

Consequently, the slaves who were present were finally convinced that Hector is dead, that Homer is not Hector, and that there was no zombie walking around in town."

Arlene said, "May I ask what kind of fruit it was? It must have had a substance that is like a mind-altering one, or a psychedelic fruit." Walt said, "It was a fruit that tasted great but with a powerful active chemical compound that mimics Dimethyltryptamine (DMT). This fruit was mainly found in Africa. The slaves knew it as an evil fruit growing in the woods, and in the part of the woods where Homer gathered the fruit is the no-return woods. Homer was told by the other slaves not to go into the woods. If he goes, he will not be back. Naira, the voodoo queen, warned him also not to go. They strongly believed there was an evil spirit in the woods that diverts people and makes them lose their way back home and wander in the woods till they succumbed to exhaustion.

Homer went and found the wild fruit. Knowing what it was, he did not eat it. He did not get high. Therefore, he found his way back.

In the months to come, there was a class of cocktail addicts walking in the streets of Little River. A colonist was so disturbed. He climbed a coconut tree while he was naked. He refused to come down. He believed he could fly. Finally, to prevent him from hurting himself, his slave had to climb to rescue him because he was going to jump down. The freedmen believed that the secret was nothing but the wine Homer used to make the cocktail. No one knew about the fruit.

Eventually, the slaves had a break because their masters became more tolerant, for the cocktail made them mellow."

Arlene concluded by saying, "How is this story related to your situation?" Walt replied, "One should never despair. I was a slave, and I was always thinking of a way out. If I could drug my oppressors to get my freedom, I would. It is an easy and painless way to do it. That is why I like the story whether it was true or not. This is the story of a smart man. If he killed, he would be dead." Arlene replied, "Of course, a white man would place his white knee on his neck and suffocate him."

Arlene commented, "Now, Walt, you must focus on getting your life together. I know you are trying to reconnect with your past and your friends. That is good, but stay away from relationships for now. The virus is not gone, and at your age, you are vulnerable. Moreover, you must think about your financial status, which is especially important before you engage in any relationship. I am sure you are one hundred percent service-connected. You had a couple of surgeries while in the service, right? What have you done exactly?" Walt said, "I know I cannot father children. Also, my appendix and my spleen were removed. I have no gallbladder." "Oh my God! You had all the 'tomy' in the book: vasectomy, splenectomy, appendectomy, and cholecystectomy." "Oh, that's how they are called," said Walt smiling. In a sad tone of voice, Arlene admitted, "I am so sorry, brother. You went through all that, alone, away from your loved ones. The government owes you big. You should be ready to collect."

"Well, I should get going. Remember, take your time. Everything will fall into place. Thank God you have two sons. Keep up, brother," Arlene uttered as she was leaving.

Philadelphia State Correctional

It is 1999. Will Saint-John has been in prison for ten months, falsely accused of raping a white adolescent girl. He is at the Philadelphia state penitentiary and is in a deep state of depression. He could not take any more of prison life without hope of freedom. He could not make sense of the world. For the first time, he has lost his faith in everything. He stopped praying and listened to the prison chaplain. It is Sunday afternoon. His father came to visit him right after church to bring him the best news. He hugged him and said joyfully, "God has answered my prayer." Will anxiously asked, "How, father? What just happened to make you say that?" Leon Saint-John (his father) replied, "It is all over the news. You are innocent, my son. Sara Manchester was pregnant because of the rape. If she were raped by a black man, her baby would be a mulatto. In her case, the child is purely a white baby." Will was stunned. He did not even know that Sara was pregnant. It was a big secret. She ran away when her father threatened to make her give up the baby for adoption right after birth. Will got excited and said to his father, "Are you sure of all that? How do you know?" Leon said, "It is in the paper. I could tell you the whole story, but my priority now is to have you home where you belong, and your lawyer is working on it. You will read more about it soon. It is in the newspaper. Sara Manchester has the baby. She came out of hiding and stated that it was her father who forced her to say her assailant was a black man, even though he wore a mask. Sara insisted that he was not you, but the father told her that it is either she complied or you will disappear for good. So, Sarah agreed to accuse you."

"Is that the truth?" The father replied, "That is all I know." And Will said, "Am I free?" And he burst into tears, "I am free. I can dispose of this orange jumpsuit, walk out of this awful place, and walk down the street again as a freeman. God, was it necessary for me to go through all that? If it was, what was the purpose? One guilty man is still at large while an innocent one was in chain. Is that justice, and am I supposed to understand?" His father said, "Will, my son, try to focus on the positive. Forget what you do not understand. Nobody fully understands God. We know he is there. That is the most important. We cannot doubt his presence nor forget it. But do not question his actions."

Will's lawyer is rejoicing about the news that Sara's baby boy is purely white. He made the motion to set his client free. Subsequently, the police reopened the case in search of the real violator.

Sara, now eighteen, pressed charges against her father who made her commit perjury and made her feel guilty for accusing a friend of a crime he did not commit. "He is the only black in this neighborhood. He has to be the one who attacked you." This statement from her father has been haunting her. Will was a student in a nearby high school. They crossed paths every day going to school. Will is particularly good at art and exceptionally good at drawing. On a few occasions, he helped Sara with her art projects and even science projects. Their friendship was genuine, but Sara's father, although religious, resented their friendship. He could not display his racism because of his wife who stood against it and the black nanny that has been in the family for a long time.

Across the street from the Manchesters is an Italian family, the Castelli. There lived an English nursemaid called Irene Connor who came as a baby nurse but never left. She has become a part of the Castelli family. She harbored a secret about Richard Castelli, the youngest of the Castelli family. She loved him like a son. She was a spinster who had left England to never return. She spent most of her life with the Castellis because of her attachment to the boy he nursed as an infant. She knew who was responsible for the crime but kept it as secret. She accidentally found a ski mask just like the one Sara described, in a bag in the attic, while looking for a bottle of wine. She questioned Ricky who confessed that it was him who attacked Sara. He stated, "I love her very much, but I don't know how to show it." Irene was in shock and found herself in a real dilemma. He scolded the boy for his action, but the secret was kept between them. Not even the parents were partaking.

Irene concealed the mask. She did not have the courage to turn Rick to the police. He is like a son to her. She made Rick her sole heir and responsible for her long-term care. To Richard Castelli's name, he had signed her house in England and some of her savings to be sure that Ricky will keep her in his family instead of sending her to a nursing home when she got old.

The ski was to remind Rick of what Irene had done for him (keeping the secret) and what crime he had committed against her childhood friend (Sara).

When the news of a baby arrived, Irene feels that Ricky should have a right to the child. In that regard, she wanted to disclose the truth to the parents about the rape, but Ricky opposed and warned her not to do so. Because doing so will incriminate her, making her an accessory to a crime, Irene kept her silence.

Louise Braxton on her side had a story to tell. Before she left Manchester's household, she made a surprising discovery. One day, she was in her room reading a magazine. From her window, she saw Ruth Manchester, the matriarch, coming out with a bag. She carefully placed it in the trash and then cover it with another bag of trash like she was hiding it. Louise became curious, and shortly after, she went to the trash and picked up the bag. She opened it and saw it was a white supremacist clan costume. Part of it was burned and there was a small bloodstain on it. She was terrified by her discovery and so disappointed. She believed in this family, because to her, it was the ideal Christian family. They were nice folks, but Vince Manchester was a racist. Facing that realization, two days later, Louise left her position as a governess, stating that if a black boy is falsely accused, she could be next. She mistakenly thought that faith in God could break all barriers. On a Friday of the month of July, early in the morning, she walked out of the Manchester's heading back home to Georgia. Ruth and the grown-up children were saddened by her departure, but Vince Manchester did not show much emotion. He was still mad that his daughter was raped by a black man. It was not much of the rape that bothered him but the criminal's background (black).

CHAPTER 11

A few months later, Louise decided to pull a prank on Ruth Manchester. She placed the costume in a box and mailed it to Vince Manchester with a typewritten note, "We are on tonight. See you around. White supremacy."

Ruth received the box that was mailed from Philadelphia with no return address. She opened it and was startled. She did not want her children to see the box. Ruth was troubled. She knows the costume was disposed of. How in the world did it found its way back to her? Who took it? She had no idea nor she suspected Louise that was too farfetched. She burned it right away and remained bewildered.

At last, in the wake of that rape incident, Sara wrote to Will to explain the circumstances that made her accuse him. Will had found some consolation from the letter, mostly for the fact that Vince Manchester was doing times in jail.

Two years later, Sara was invited to a Christmas party at the Castelli's. She attended with her son, a toddler then. He was the star of the party. Irene brought to Rick's attention that the boy has a birthmark on the occipital area of his head, just like the one on Rick's head. Rick was already fascinated by the baby. He had brought him many presents for Sara and the boy. Eric and Angelini Castelli found the resemblance to Rick rather uncanny. The parents were troubled. They did not know what to think while they feared for the ugly truth. Could their son be the rapist, or could Sara and Rick be lovers long before the rape? Irene stated that the little boy is Rick's son and declared that Sara was not raped because, when she was ten years old, she caught her and Rick having sex. They claimed that they were playing husband and wife. Rick must acknowledge his son. So, Irene declared. Eric said, "Do you know that he can go to prison for years? What is more important in this situation? His son or his freedom? What good it does to have a son and you are not free to raise him?" Angelini started crying and spoke, "I knew something was wrong. Rick was disturbed and highly anxious after the story broke, overly concerned. He was continually inquiring about Sara. So, that is what was bothering him, his conscience. What should we do? Make him confess to Sara? Who knows? They were children together. They liked each other. What evil spirit came on to Rick? He is a shy boy. How can I turn him to the police?"

Irene said, "Never, nobody will turn him to the police. We need a strategy to soften Sara's heart. We need to convene to put a plan in motion." "I am sending Rick to Italy to school. Time will calm things down," Eric declared. Angelini said, "How cowardly of you, Rick. Is that the best solution you can come up with? Make him run away from his mistakes, with no reproof, no lecture to him, nothing, just a passport and let him go? Is that your idea of good parenting?" Eric said, "But what other options do we have? Turn him to the police? I cannot do that because rape is a serious crime. He goes to jail, his life will be over." Irene said, "We must talk to Sara in his behalf." Angelini said, "No, Rick must confess himself to Sara. Not us, he is not a minor. He should take responsibility for his actions. His father wants to send him away without digging for the cause of his behavior. Italy will not change him. What if he assails another girl in Italy? Then, where will he escape to? Our son needs a psychoanalyst. He really needs psychological help now before it is too late."

The next day, the Castellis confronted their son who candidly admitted being the violator and coincidentally the father of Sara's little boy, Brian. He sounded very remorseful and intended to confess to the parish priest. Irene reminded him that clergies are not to be trusted in such a case and it would be a bad move, a big mistake. She stated that even though the clergy must keep secrecy, when someone else is falsely accused of a crime, taking the blame for someone else, the clergy most likely will break his silence. "Especially the black priest there, he would not give you absolution. I assure you that. For the fact that a black man had already paid for your offense, justice must prevail always." To conclude, the mother recommended that Rick confess to Sara instead.

Will was out of prison and started a new life with his girlfriend. One day, he was visited by the police who wanted to extract a DNA specimen. He asked them, "Why My DNA? The child is white." The police replied, "Standard procedure to establish the baby's paternity." Will surprisingly made a stunning remark that changed the course of the investigation. He said, "If you are really looking for the baby's father, why not swab all the young male friends of Sara? I was not the only male friend she had. How about his closest neighbor Rick Castelli? I heard the baby looks just like him with a birthmark on the back of his head. Does not that count for something? Matthew Callahan, Jeffrey Preston, Michael Barnes, they are all her classmates and friends. Should you go after them too?"

The police took note and started to investigate other young men in Sara's neighborhood.

When a local paper announced that all the boys who were neighbors to the Manchester family submit a DNA test to confirm the baby's paternity, the Castellis had a serious concern—their son, Rick, will be exposed and even go to prison.

In the light of that, Rick rushed to confess to Sara. Sara was torn. She wept and fell on her knees asking God, "Why are so many negativities around me? What should I do in the middle of such a difficult conundrum? I was forced to falsely accuse a young man because he was black and he went to prison. Subsequently, I sent my father to jail. Now, another man deserves to go to prison because of me. I am sending men to prison and standalone with a child in my arms. How much can my heart take? How do I turn the father of my child to the police? How do I forgive myself for sending Will to prison? How do I forget my father for what he did? Conclusively, it is not only the rape that bothers but also all the circumstances around it. Rick is the violator, but I have known him all my life. He is my confidant, my childhood playmate. How can I send him to prison? I do not deserve to live but I must, because of my son.

Should I thank God for something? Yes, the rapist is not a stranger. For that reason, I must forgive Rick and drop the case against him. God will judge him as seen fit. Would not be that the hardest thing to explain to a child? I sent your father to prison, your grandfather to prison, and an innocent man to prison?

At last, now, my son is no longer the son of nobody. He has a father. Against all that others have to say, I cannot send another man to prison. The police can stop their investigation. Why did not they do it before Will went to prison? They listened to my father and did not look for any proof or evidence. They just condemned Will."

Sara's lawyer made the motion to drop the charge and so the police could close the case.

Ruth Manchester visited her husband in jail. It was her first time visiting a prison. She did not like the experience—she had to remove her jewelry, she could not keep her pocketbook, she needed quarters to lock her stuff, and she had to be scanned. It was not an easy process nor a pleasant experience. Her husband was called. He showed no sign of remorse for what he did. Instead, he was complaining about life in prison and how unhappy he was. "Did you hear from my lawyer, Ruth? I cannot stand it any longer here."

Ruth replied, "You sent Will to prison for almost a year, didn't you? You really took me for a fool. You made my daughter lie under oath and threatened to have Will disappear if she did not collaborate with your lies. How do you sleep at night knowing fully that you coerced her to lie and you kept it all from me? I trusted you as a new man, a Christian. I was so wrong and naïve to think that you have changed. I even tried to destroy your white supremacist costume, but it came back to you. Somebody in the neighborhood knows about you being a white supremacist." Vince said, "What are you talking about?" "Someone sent you an invitation to come out to spread terror, like in the past. How would the children feel to find out that you, a faithful member of the church, is a radical white supremacist?"

"I am not listening to all your blab blab. I want to get out of here." Ruth calmly added, "The violator was not a young black man after all. It was a white one, one that we know." Vince's facial expression changed quickly, and he asked, "Who are you referring to?" Ruth responded, "Our neighbor, Sara's friend, Richard Castelli. He is also the father of the baby. What do you have to say about that?" "The police are making that up. Rick would never do such a thing. Whites do not usually involve in crimes like that. That is a lie," he declared. Ruth said, "The baby looks like Rick and he confessed, so, who or what are you defending here exactly? A rapist can be a man of any race, any social class, except that it cannot be a woman." And Vince inquired, "How did he confess? What did he say to defend himself?"

"When the news broke out that all males in our neighborhood were required to submit a specimen for DNA testing to establish the baby's paternity once and for all and prosecute the offender, Rick freaked out. He rushed to write to Sara. I found the letter. I was curious, so I opened it gently, read it, made a copy, and closed the envelope." Vince said, "You never change. You like to read other people's letters, to mingle in everybody's business. Read the damned letter for me." He did not say much. "I am the guilty one. I am Brian's father because it was me who assaulted you after the school party. I was jealous of Will. I couldn't stand you being fond of him. You were often talking about him being smart and all that. I felt like I was walking in his shadow. You and I are friends since we were young. I could not control my anger. So, instead of attacking Will, I assailed you.

Since that event, I am troubled. I know you will never see me as Rick again, but a monster, a rapist. It was my dream that one day I will marry you. But now, my life, my future, all is in your hand. 'I am sorry' will not make it because it is not strong enough to express how terrible I feel. I will be forever a broken man, a man with a shadowy past.

No matter who I will become in the future, nothing will make me whole again. And then, there is my son who sooner or later will be told about the sin of the father (his father). Will he despise me, or will he forgive me? I do not know. God has forgiven me because I have made atonement, I am contrite, but men will not forgive me and that is something I have to learn to live with because I must go on living."

Vince said, "Beautiful letter, very touching, he sounds remorseful. I still cannot believe he did that once again. It was because of this boy Will. All comes back to Will. That is what happened when you mix up with the wrong group. Melting pot, I hate melting pot." Ruth said, "You are the greatest hypocrite that ever lived. You used to lead prayers in the church. The blacks in the church trust you and you feel that way. You make me want to spew." Vince continued saying, "At least, she can keep the child and face the world with some dignity. And one more thing, when I get out of here, I will do what a father must do. Rick Castelli must marry Sara. He dishonored my daughter. I am not taking that lying down, you know." Ruth laughed and spoke, "Are you out of your mind? Don't you realize that the relationship between you and Sara is severely damaged? It is like a glass vase that is shattered into small pieces and cannot be put together again. So, Sarah is going to let you make decisions on her life? Is that so? You are losing it, Vince. You need psychological help. Let me tell you my experience with racism. I was once a racist when I was young even though my mom said that she was constantly bullied in school because she was Jewish. But all changed when I took my racism too far. I was a moron then. On one Saturday morning, I was in an open-air market with a group of friends, very prejudiced they were. Not a good group. They often said very unpleasant things about blacks, and I was part of that clique. I was in line to buy vegetables and fruits; a black woman was in front of me and I made an unpleasant remark. I murmured, 'Do I have to stand and wait behind this nigger?' She turned around, smiled, and said nicely, 'You want to buy something? Go before me, go ahead!' I quickly realized she was not American. She spoke with a heavy accent and she was also very friendly. She even said to me, 'You have beautiful eyes, you know.'

I was happy to hear such a compliment. Coming from another women, I know it was true. Nobody ever noticed my eyes before. And then she taught me about avocado and corn. She said to always squeeze the head of the avocado. If you see water, it is most likely watery. No water just the flesh, it's good, and she said, 'Let me show you good corns.' I was melted. I felt so ignorant next to her. She had class. And shortly after, as she was leaving, she looked around for me to innocently said, 'Bye nigger, bye,' with a great smile. People were in dismay and said, 'What did she call you?' A Caucasian man who was at the cashier said, 'That is outrageous. She cannot get away with that. Who does she think she is to call you nigger?' And he was about to go after her. I spoke, 'Leave her alone. She is my neighbor. She means neighbor.' In fact, she did not know the word nigger at all. She thought I said neighbor to her, so I was the villain. I learned a lot about that simple word nigger. We made it up. The real word is N- E- G- R- E which is the French translation for a black male so much so that in the Haitian creole, a beautiful woman is often called a 'bel negger.' In the French version, belle negresse or beautiful black woman. So, you see, when you use that word, you are a *cretin* which is worse than ignorant. You are genetically stupid.

Thereafter, I look for goodness in people, and I never used the word nigger in any way. I conclude that if the word nigger means ignorant, we are all ignorant in some aspect because we do not know it all. What would you do if you come from the wilderness, or from a remote area, and you never saw a modern toilet before? You are thirsty, you look around, and see the toilet bowl with fresh, clean water in it. Won't you quench your thirst? Yes, you would drink from it. Because you are ignorant, you do not know. You see clean water." Vince said, "Oh, please, that sounds disgusting."

And then he added, "By the way, whose idea was it to check all the boys in the neighborhood?" Ruth said, "Will's lawyer, because by standing procedure, although the child looks white, since Will was accused as the violator, he had gone through the paternity test process." "What did Sara say about Rick?" Ruth said, "I handed her the letter. She did not say anything to me. I do not know what she decided to do. It is going to take time for Sarah to get back on her feet again. Can you imagine how embarrassed she must have felt at the party when everybody was asking, 'How come this baby looks like Rick?'? Her heart was twisted between doubt. Did she sleep with Rick? And trust, it could not be Rick who violated her. Anyway, I encouraged her to go back to school, to fulfill her dream of becoming a professional nurse while I will look over the baby. She is all broken up and alone. All that is because of you, and if you think that being classified as a racist is cool, think again. If one day you realized that the CEO of your company, the one who is signing your check is a black man, what would you do? Frankly, if I were not a Christian, I would divorce you on the spot, not for racism, but for what you did to Sarah. Rick raped her physically, but you, you did the same emotionally and that is despicable. You remind me of a loathsome human being by the name of Adolf Hitler."

Vince said, "He was a great leader. He gave Germany back its greatness." "At the expense of the Jews, he was nothing but a coward, an insecure son of a bitch who was jealous of the Jews for they were smart and wealthy. He destroyed so many lives, based on race, claiming that Germany must be pure white. Are you a pure white, Vince? Am I going to check your DNA to see what will come up?" Ruth declared and Vince responded, "What will that do? Both of my parents were white. I have nothing to be ashamed of. I am proud of my race and I want to protect it at any course. There is nothing wrong with that. By the way, did Louise know about my costume? She is probably the one pulling a prank on me." Ruth said, "How do you know it is a prank? 'We will be on tonight' signed by the white supremacist. You call that a prank? Louise did not know about that. That is shameful. Why would I let her know that you are a Klux? She would not work for us. Tell me, Vince, how did you feel when praying in the church? I saw you laying your hands on those colored peoples' heads, praying for them. How did you do that? Did you really pray for them or did you curse them instead? May God have mercy on your miserable soul." "You talk too much, Ruth. Did you tell Louise about my past as a Klux member? Since she was more of your friend than your housekeeper—watching soap operas together, going to the casinos together, you even took her on a cruise with the children. She does your hair instead of you going to the beauty salon. I have never seen a white person who trusted a black servant as you did. Do you have low self-esteem or something? I could easily afford an English nanny, like the Castelli. But you insisted on hiring a black nanny. There was role confusion there. Was she a governess, or a friend? I watched you through the years. She had domination on you. You listened to her advice more than you did to mine, and I resented her for that privilege. I tried hard to conceal it for the sake of the children who were smitten by her. Nanny Lou as they surnamed her. My children would be much prouder to have a white nanny since they are white. Does not that make sense to you, Ruth?"

She replied, "No, Vince, it does not make sense because the children were happy with Nanny Lou, and let me refresh your memory. During colonial times, it was a black woman who nursed babies and watched them grow and develop. Your ancestors were rocked as infants by those black women's arms and hands. Even if they were in bondage, they would sing their made-up lullaby to put them to sleep. You resented her mostly because you had to pay. If it were free, she was a slave, and you would not have such a concern. You just prove to me that you will never change. You do not have a shred of regret. You do not look a bit remorseful for your negative attitude and behavior toward others. Oh, Vince, you, once the love of my life, how estrange have you become. It seems that I never knew you. Consequently, when you get back home, you will have a separate room and we will have separate lives. The good grass and the weed cannot grow together. The weed usually takes over. My mother was a Jewish woman. Why in the world did I marry you? Do you know, Vince? Maybe because my father was Irish, just like you. So, I found a mutuality. You reminded me of my father that I loved dearly. I am going back home now. Should I say goodbye or hail Hitler?"

Vince asked, "Ruth, are you in your right state of mind? Do you not want to hold me and hug me before you leave? You are my wife, and you are rejecting me for those people." Ruth said, "No, not for the black people, but because you are a true villain. Next time you have a shave, ask the barber to shape your mustache like the Fuhrer's since you laud him as being a great leader, even today, when the world anathematizes him." Vince said sadly, "So, that is it? You and I are through? Seemingly, I cannot stand for what I believe in. About Hitler and the Jews, your people would do just like Hitler to defend their religion because they live for Judaism. But for me, I cannot defend my race."

Ruth answered, "Faith and race are two different matters. Let me explain. There is reason to stand for your faith because there is always an incentive. There is hope for something great at the end. Race does not offer anything at all. It is like fighting for a bone that has no meat on, and no marrow in it, a hollow bone. Race is nothing but a group of people with similar physical features, that is all. Sending an innocent man to prison is more than racism. It is hatred."

Vince said, "I heard you, you do have a point, and it is my turn to lecture you, Ruth. In reference to Louise, you chose her to work for you, not so much because you love blacks, but because you stereotyped them, thinking tis the kind of job black women do and they are cheaper. Moreover, you would have more control over them than white ones. Knowing you, you would never hire a white woman by fear of competition. Isn't that the truth?" Ruth responded, "What a ridiculous idea. You do not make sense anymore." Vince chuckled, saying, "Ridiculous but true." And Ruth continued, "I must say you are a charming man, but you have a sinister side, a side that I have never known. You were once a clan member, you left the clan, but you kept its ideology and you acted on it. So, why did you exit the clan? To marry me I suppose and pretend to be a faithful Christian. You fooled me, alright, but you cannot fool God. Goodbye, Vince, take care of yourself." "Ruthey, do not go like that, honey!" he begged. Ruth returned to murmur, "You need to do atonement for what you did."

Ruth saw Angelini, Rick's mother, coming out of her house. She looked sad and depressed. So, Ruth called her. The two mothers met for the first time since Rick has confessed. Angelini said to Ruth, "I don't think you would even talk to me. I have no spoken word to describe or to express how I feel inside." She broke into tears. "I am so ashamed. Where did I go wrong as a parent? I have been on my knees praying. Where did my prayers go? What did they do? Am I praying the wrong way?"

Ruth replied, "I feel your pain. I have no spoken words to console you, but God has the power to heal. Our families will be healed. It is not the time to lose faith. It is the time to look inside ourselves and see what is really wrong with us. I need to fast to get God's attention." Angelini said, "What does that do? People do it all the time." Ruth said, "I don't do it all the time. That is why God will notice me before those who do it all the time. I am in my hour of need. My daughter is broken up. My husband is a mess. You need to do the same, Angelini. Change the way you pray. For once, put the rosary down. Go to God in the name of Jesus. He is the only mediator between you and God. No Mother Mary, no Paul, no Peter, or Jude and Joseph for they were all mortals, like you and me. We do not know where they are right now, do we? Listen, Angie, I have nothing against them. Think about this. Suppose you have the choice of choosing between the vice president and your congressman to link you to the president, which one would choose? The vice-president or your congressman?" Angie said, "The vice-president of course." "So, you get my point."

CHAPTER 12

Angie asked, "How do you feel about Rick?" "I still like him. He seemed to be contrite and remorseful. However, he needs counseling to let an innocent young man take the blame and go to prison. That is hard to forget, but in time, we all will find solace. Do not despair, Angie, you are a mother. I know exactly how you are feeling, but do not despair. I don't hold anything against your family or your son."

* * *

In a Philadelphia prison, two men were engaged in a heated argument. A new detainee was screaming, "Jesus, son of God, have mercy on me." A Muslim detainee got really annoyed and said, "Be quiet, there is no such thing as a son of God. The true God has no son, no wife. If you want a God with sons and daughters, go to Hinduism or reach out to the so-called Greco or Roman gods, like Zeus and Poseidon and all. Only pagan gods have wives, children, and even concubines. The real God is different from all pagan ones. As you can see, they all died. But he remains. He does not share power with any other God. He is the one and only true God of the universe. Jesus was a messenger of God, an envoy. He was created by God. What is so hard to understand, you so-called Christians? You are getting on my damn nerves, man." The other man said sarcastically, "Oh, Mr., forgive me twelve hundred times for my ignorance. By the way, twelve hundred is the amount of your stimulus check." "Are you trying to make fun of me?" said the other guy. "It is not intentional. My name is Charles Lester. I am talking about the God of Jesus Christ, of Abraham, and all." The other replied, "My name is Nadim and I am a Muslim." Charles said, "I fear Allah. I was not referring to the god of ISIS, the Taliban, of Boca Haram with the two hundred girls, the god of Hezbollah, Hamas, and the god of sharia laws. I am even afraid of being in the same room with you, sir, because you can see me as an infidel and destroy me." Another prisoner was laughing and saying, "Why you two do not go outside in the street to set your score? I am tired of your lousy argument about religion." Everybody laughed saying, "Yeah, go outside, get out of this facility, go in the street to fight for your beliefs." Nadim said, "Charles, are you crazy?" He replied, "Not that I know of. Maybe I am, but I have never been diagnosed." Nadim added, "What made you mention twelve hundred. Don't you find that irrelevant?" Charles declared, "Money is never irrelevant, Nadim. Have not you heard your uncle will send you a check for twelve hundred dollars to compensate for what this antisocial virus called corona has done to us?" "Where do you get your information?" Nadim inquired. Charles replied, "From the news. Do not you watch TV or read the newspapers? Come on! Man, take a break from reading the Quran, read some other stuff, brother, and get enlightened. Big bucks are coming your way. Make sure you don't die of COVID before your stimulus arrived."

A prisoner commented, "I do not get it. One moment, those two men were arguing. Now, look at them, talking about the stimulus check. Money brings them together." Another prisoner said, "It was Nadim that was heated up. Charles was having fun. I know him. He is a standup comedian. Nobody recognized him since he has a mask on. It is Charles Bailey." He said, "Lester, be incognito, but it is unmistakably Charles Bailey, the comedian. It is easy to detect the comic style, for example: Boca Haram has two hundred girls, hey! That is not relevant to the subject. He was making a joke."

"Speaking of jokes, my situation sounds like a joke, but it is not," stated an inmate called Andrew Alexander. "Today, I was supposed to meet the judge, but I asked my lawyer to reschedule and find me another judge." Somebody replied loudly, "Are you joking? You are a privileged prisoner. You can choose your judge? Tell us why you do not want this judge." Andrew explained, "When I was growing up, in south Philadelphia, I had two friends. We were always together, from elementary to high school. We loved to play cowboys or police. I always wanted to be the villain because it was more exciting, yields more fun than the nice character. My two other buddies played sheriff and judge and alternatively. But me, I was always the bandit.

After high school, I went to a vocational school and my two friends. One went to the police academy and the other to college. In time, we lost track of each other. Until one day, I got arrested by the one who became a police officer. He did not recognize me, but I saw his name and face. There was no doubt. It was him. I was too ashamed to let him know it was me. It was when I presented my identification that he looked at me and said, 'Andy! Oh my God! Andy!' He was shocked to see me. He could not help it. He sobbed and called another officer to process my arrest. Coincidentally, I heard my counselor said who my judge is. He is the other friend. What is that? Is it destiny, fate, coincidence? Is there a meaning to that?"

"Oh brother, brother, how fascinating is your little story. By the way, what is the name of the judge if I may ask?" "Rudolph Pemberton, the judge. The police is Hayden Stanford." "Wow! That is odd. How coincidental. You could not arrange a plot like that even if you wanted to, but it happens by chance. Life is a master planner." An inmate commented, "I remembered Hayden saying to me, 'I have been looking for you, for years, pal.'" Andrew uttered, "Well, that is what happens when you are reduced to the lowest term. Do not you all remember that, in arithmetic, you would get an F for not reducing your fraction to the lowest term? I must admit that I am now reduced to my lowest term. I am in a dark place right now. I cannot face the judge who used to be a comrade. It would be hard on him putting him in an awkward position to judge me, a childhood friend." Nadim who was listening to him sighed and said, "Dark places can get lighted up. It would be hopeless to be at the threshold of the black hole. By the way, what brings you here?"

He responded, "Selling stolen goods. That is the charge. An old acquaintance of mine called me to offer some cheap merchandise. I went to his house and saw that his garage was filled with various types of merchandise: designer clothes, shoes, jewelry, firecrackers, coats, a lot of stuff. He told me that he needs to liquidate some merchandise because he needs to raise money fast. He needed a fix badly and owed a drug dealer some money. If I gave him one thousand bucks, I could have as much merchandise as I wanted. At the time, it sounded like a good venture, a good deal for me. So, I asked no question, I gave the money, and I took some stuff. Three days later, he was arrested. His house was raided and he told the police that he sold some merchandise to me. So, the police came after me. They saw me leaving the driveway. They followed me and then stopped me to search my car. So, they saw some merchandise in my car trunk. That is my story." One man said, "I always wanted to wear a big Cuban link chain made of gold. Do you have any at home?" They howled and one of them asked, "Why do you want a chain when you are already in a chain?" That sounded funny. Everybody laughed.

Andrew said, "No, they took everything they suspected was stolen. My wife left me. She warned me not to deal with that man. I did not listen." "We are sorry all that happens to you, Andrew, but better days are on the horizon, the sun will shine again. Every chain has its cross, they said. Yep, we keep telling us that even if it is not true. We got to have hope," declared Bill, one of the prisoners.

Bill added, "Your story reminds me of my childhood friends. I had three friends, two boys my age and a girl, older than me. Her name was Virginia. I have no idea where Virginia is today. If she is alive or dead, I do not know. The three of us had one problem in common. Our parents were not married, Catholic church policy, parents must be religiously married for their children to partake in communion. And as children, we thought communion was a big deal. We wanted to partake like other children, but we could not. When we were about twelve years old, we talked to our parents about getting married. They said that as far they are concerned, they were married before God. We did not understand.

My father explained to me that marriage is about committing to each other faithfully, not going to church or in front of a mayor. That makes marriage. Fidelity is marriage. So, they were not about to get married at all.

One day, my friend John and I decided to pull a trick. We were going to do something to make them get married, but we could come up with what to do. Virginia who was a little older told me and John how her parents got married. She told us that she was about to run away from home when suddenly, her mother got the flu. Virginia had already packed a bag to go when she learned that her mother was hospitalized.

She gave up the idea, but we picked it up and made a plan to run away. Virginia mentioned that she was not going too far. She would have gone hiding in the church tribune. Anyway, Virginia's mom became so sick. Her husband called the priest to give her the last rite. The older sister, Jennie, begged her father to marry her mother before she passed. The father agreed and the priest married her in the hosp. She was dressed in a nice gown. Miraculously, Emma survived the flu. She pulled through after a couple of days. The children rejoiced. Consequently, Virginia received her first communion. So, we heard the story, we made our plan. One day after school, we did not go home. The news was out. Our pictures were on the papers. They were looking for us. Virginia went to the church and found us. She brought us food. Then, we gave her a note to drop at our parent's house. The note said, 'Get married and we will be home. You are living in sins.' They sent us the answer through the newspaper: the missing children's parents are getting married, so, they can come back home. We heard of that, then we left the church and came home. A month later, our parents were married at Capernaum on the wedding day at Capernaum, big parties for the collective wedding.

Today, I am here, but John my buddy is a priest. Since he was a boy, he wanted to be a priest. He particularly loved the priest costume. He grew up with the dream and concretize it. I dreamed to be a minister. I would love to immerse people in the water, to baptize them, but somewhere, I drifted away from my goal. I got married early and had a bunch of children, unable to keep a job due to a back problem. Now I am here on a charge of firearm possession without a permit. I rarely go to church. I seldom think of God and that's even worse than not going to church. It means you ignore him.

Why am I like that? I have so much in my mind. It seems like it was yesterday John and I were talking about our parents, how they expressed their love for each other. John used to say, 'My dad loves my mom. He washes her panties, her bras, her stocking, and lines them dry. My mom always cooked my dad his favorite foods, press his shirts before he lives for work, and he always kisses her in her mouth. You see, they are married. They love each other. Why can't I get communion?' And I would say, 'My mom loves my dad. She is his barber. She does cut his hair, trim his mustache, and sit on him sometimes to kiss him. My dad sometimes called her, "Honey, come eat with me. I don't like to eat alone." She used to say, "I would do more than that, James. I am coming to feed you. Have your mouth wide open." You see, they love each other, so they are married.' That was our humble way of thinking. Today, I miss my childhood, me who wanted to grow up so bad, but now that I am an adult, I enjoy my past more than the present. As for my future, it does not seem to be brighter. So, I linger in the yesteryears." Andrew said, "Well, it does not hurt to relive your past." Charles said, "The past is sometimes sweeter than the present."

Andrew wanted to know why Charles Lester was arrested. So, he inquired, "Charles, what did you do exactly to be arrested?" "It may sound funny, but it is a serious matter. How crazy everything is now with that coronavirus. Imagine, I was scheduled to go on a cruise. I went to board my ship where I was supposed to, in New York. To my surprise, when I got on board, I saw a crowd of sick people carrying a portable oxygen tank. They were in hospital gowns. A security guard threw a gown at me, telling me to put it on. After that, someone took my temperature. I felt something was off and I was confused, so I questioned, 'Is this cruise ship going to Labadie?' Someone exclaimed, 'Labadie! This is Corona ship, going to Corvid island, your destination.' I murmured, 'What?' And I kept repeating, 'Corvid Island, my destination. What does that mean?' He rudely replied, 'Because you are positive and symptomatic, you must be sent to Corvid island. Not enough hospital beds in US to keep all of you in quarantine. There, on the island, you will stay till you die. However, if you make it through, you will come back home. Is that understood? Besides, if you were going on a cruise, where is your luggage?' I replied nicely, 'It was all-inclusive. There is no need for luggage, just my backpack.' Everybody around laughed. Some of them could not even laugh without coughing. They sounded awful and then I realized that I was at risk. I had no mask.

I declared loudly, 'But I am sorry, I am in the wrong ship. I am not sick yet.' The guard replied, 'Really, and why aren't you wearing a mask? Aren't you afraid of COVID-19?' He stuttered as he spoke. I responded sarcastically, 'I am already in a black outfit. Adding a mask will make me look like a bandit. I am not Zorro.' He said to another police, 'He talks too much, no time for jokes. Take him away.' Then, a police officer grabbed me to take me inside a cabin as a sick person. Then, I resisted the arrest. He put me on my belly, his foot on my back, while other police proceeded to handcuff me. He pushed so hard on my back I began to fart loud, and the odor was offensive. Then he got mad, saying that is disrespectful. I spoke, 'I am sorry, officer. Last night, I had a big bowl of baked beans, onion rings, and broccoli. So, what to expect, officer, and you are the one pushing hard on my belly. You made me pass wind and I am sorry. Please, officer, have mercy on me so God will have mercy on you for all your wrongdoings. Jesus, please, have mercy on me. Officer, please let me go.' He stopped torturing me and brought me here on the charge of 'failure to wear a mask.' How ridiculous!" "Well, you are lucky to be alive. He could have placed his foot on your neck and get the life out of you," Andrew commented.

* * *

Ruth received Vince's DNA test result. The result is so troubling that she doubted it. However, the lab reassured her that their results are ninety-nine percent accurate. She invited her children to read what presents a puzzle in the result. The children, three of them, Jennie, Hansel, and Sara, are baffled by what the test revealed. Their father has Irish, Polish, Egyptian, German, Russian, Jewish, and one percent from Madagascar relations. But the mind-blowing fact is that Vince has two half-brothers and a few half-nephews and nieces from Jamaica, half-brothers who are mulattos. Vince is not interested in the result, but Ruth is looking for answers. She feels that there is a secret in the family. Nobody had ever mentioned any connection with Jamaica except every year, a case of Jamaican rum arrived from Jamaica where he ordered from a distillery called Mahoney Distilleries. He claimed that is one of the best rums. That is all she knows but Ruth will not let go. She called Vince's uncle, Albert Manchester, the oldest in the family to explain what she thinks is a discrepancy in the test.

Albert, at first, hesitated to break the family's secret, but he thought that he is the only one alive. All the Manchester sisters and brothers died. So, it is about time for the secret to be out. Ruth ought to know what secret is kept in the family she married into. On that note, he came to visit Ruth to clarify the test result. Ruth and her children were waiting for him. He arrived and they welcomed him. He started by telling Ruth that what he is about to reveal has nothing to do with her. Except, she was kept in the dark because Vincent her husband has no clue of what secret is kept within his family. Albert explained, "All started with Samuel, our eldest brother, who went to invest financially in Jamaica when he was young. There, he met a young woman who helped him settle in a strange land. She was his manager, his right-hand woman, and eventually, his lover. Of that relationship, two boys were conceived.

My brother did what he had to do. He legally gave his name to the two boys: Daniel and Dylan Manchester. He lived in Jamaica for many years. The mother of the children fell in love with another man who wanted to marry her. Angelucia married another man, leaving my brother with a broken heart. All that was because Angie had watched a picture about slavery. She saw the tortures, the mistreatment, and mental abuse the blacks from Africa suffered. She was deeply affected and that changed their relationship. She stated that even though she loves Samuel, she would not feel comfortable marrying him, not because of his race but of history. So, they went separate ways. Later, my brother left Jamaica, came back to the state, and chose a wife, Martha Sterling, Vincent and Jason's mother. When Samuel died, his estate in Jamaica was still managed by Angelucia. The two boys had their share of inheritance according to Samuel's will.

Martha declared that her children will not inherit or share a last name with the two boys. She will rather pay them off to give up the Manchester name. She wanted to have no part with the Jamaican boys who will spoil her sons, making them smoke weeds and have dread and eventually, will turn out to be nothing. She said she did not want any reggae singer and marijuana user in the family. So, she went to Jamaica. I chaperoned her in the trek, not that I encouraged her attitude and action. I told her she was wrong, but she would not listen to me. I went with her by curiosity. I really wanted to see Angelucia's reaction to that offer. 'Give up the name for lands.' I was pleased that I went. Watching those two women head-to-head, I got a good kick out of it. Today, I am a witness to their confrontation.

She wrote first to her explaining what she wanted. Then, she went to have papers drawn by a lawyer to give all the lands owned by Samuel to his two sons and her. She would have the rum and sugar industries which were the real moneymakers. In Martha's mind, Angelucia is not a brilliant person. She is a black bimbo, not smart enough to fight her. When those two ladies met in Kingston, Jamaica, it was a turbulent encounter. Martha had no idea what she was bargaining for. Angelucia came with her lawyer well-prepared to give up the name but at a high cost and Martha could not back off.

Angelucia told her, 'Of all the good characters in the bible, you chose to be Sara, a conniving woman who used a poor slave and then sent her away in the wilderness with her son and vase of water. That story is in the bible as information, not a recommendation. So, you think you are Sara, I am Agar, and my children are not good enough to even carry the name of their biological father. That is an insult. I hate you for it. However, I am not Agar. I will not just walk away with my boys and nothing. I want the dough, a big chunk of it. I did not sleep with him and bear him two sons just for his name. Seeing that the last name Manchester means so much to you and I do not particularly believe in a name, then, you can have it, but keep in mind my sons and I will not share the wealth with you. You already told me what you want in a letter. Now, it is my turn to tell you what I want in return.

I want everything. It is either the name with half of the wealth for my sons or give up the name and take all the wealth except for the cash in the bank. That you can keep. Take it or leave it, white woman. Moreover, your son will never know about my sons. They will not meet. You predicted that they will be marijuana addicts without any purpose in life. In another word, they will be losers.

We shall see about that. God is my witness. I will make sure that my sons became CEOs of Mahoney industries, selling our products internationally. Thinking back all that you said to me, you sound very uneducated. Where did Samuel pull you from? White ghetto? You have forty-eight hours to sign the papers and get out of Jamaica, you, imbecile.' Martha responded, 'I still despise you and your sons. They are not my husband's. Keep clear of my family. Manchester is a respectable name and I want to keep it that way.' Angelucia told her, 'Why do not you go back from the dung hole you came from? Get lost!' Martha was infuriated. She was really upset. Her face was red, tears in her eyes. She could not wait to return to the state."

CHAPTER 13

"**M**artha Manchester signed the papers giving up everything to Angelucia, leaving her sons only with their father's saving account and a large sum of money from insurance and annuities. She never wanted her sons to know about Jamaica and the half-brothers. So, she kept the story a secret till today. Before I leave, Ruth, I want to show you something. Go to the bar. Bring me a rum bottle." Effectively, she went and came back with a bottle. "Here it is, the picture of Daniel and Dylan on the bottle. And this rum is Vince's favorite, unaware that is his father's brand. Forgive Vince for being a racist with hatred not only of black, for that matter for any other. He is uncomfortable with any other race. His mother raised him to be like that. Me, I am a little bit of everything, so, I am white just like I could have been black. I am sorry to disturb your peace." Everybody is silent. "What does that mean?" Ruth said, "I am speechless, I don't know what to say." Jennie said, "So, grandma is responsible for all that, giving away what is rightfully ours. We have lands and a big fortune in Jamaica, but for a matter of name, we end up with nothing. How stupid that is. Where is Angelucia?" Albert replied, "I have no idea." Sara said, "On many occasions, I found my father drinking that rum. He was always gazing at the picture of two men on the bottle. He seemed to be curious about them. Are we going to tell him all that, Mom?" Ruth responded, "Should I?" Sara said, "How about grandma? Should we confront her?"

Albert said, "You will be wasting your breath. She will tell you that Angelucia is a sorcerer who brought misfortune and evil to her family. She will never confess what she did. Especially now that her memory is half gone. She regretted her decision later when she found out that most of Samuel's investment was in Jamaica. The saddest part is Vincent has no idea. He ordered rum from the very distilleries his father developed. My brother was a savvy businessman with great vision and did not underestimate that black woman, Angie, who helped him get lands for cheap, to plant sugarcane, to get manpower. She taught him the way of life in Jamaica. She was his guardian angel and very instrumental in launching the business. So, when she left him to marry another man, that was a big blow for Sam and a setback for the business. On the rebound, Vincent married Martha and spent the rest of his life miserably with her because she was and still a control freak with a borderline personality disorder. I am sorry to be the one to bring you this story today. Let me have a drink of the Mahoney rum, please." And Jennie said, "No uncle Al, you are driving. We cannot take that responsibility. Remember, do not drink and drive." Al said, "Yeah, you have a point."

Later, Hansel asked his mother what Angelucia meant by Sara being a villain, "I thought she is a good character in the bible." Before Ruth could answer, Jennie responded, "A lot of people read that book with the idea that everyone is good in the bible. They do not take time to analyze a certain story. In Sara's story, if it is a true story, they used Agar as a surrogate mother. When Sara gave birth, she chased her, stating that her child will not inherit with her son." Hansel said, "Do you know that story creates all the chaos going on in the middle east today?" Sara exclaimed, "Today! Not just today, the bickering has been there for ages. They are all the same people who pretend to be different from each other. They are all descendants of Noah and Abraham and they are all sinners who dislike each other." Jennie said, "Sending Agar and her son away with only a jug of water is not a sign of love or compassion from Abraham and Sara, at all."

Ruth said, "The bible did not describe them as sinless humans. Anyway, today has been a great day for me. I was blind, now I see." "How do you plan to make dad see, Mom?" asked Hansel. Ruth calmly replied, "I am not thinking of that now. He will see on his own." "So, Mom, what are you thinking about?" Hansel asked with a smile and added, "You are up to something. I can feel it." Ruth murmured, "I would like to go to Jamaica to visit the sugar cane plantations, the sugar, molasses, sugar cane rum factories that once belonged to Vince's father. That is sad. He would have been part of all that. And with those two brothers, he would not be racist. He would have a chance to get to know black people better. Therefore, he would not be so bitter." Hansel said, "Why do you have to go, Mom? Forget about those things you just mentioned." "I must go visit. No one can stop me." Hansel replied, "Yeah, right, just like no one could stop Grandma Martha from going." Ruth said, "O, no, I am going to Jamaica on good terms, not to destroy a potential relationship but to establish a relationship between the Moroney brothers and your father." Sara was listening and she spoke, "Be careful, Mom, they might think you are after something." "As I said, I am going in good faith. After I explained my reasons, they will understand that I am not looking for inheritance," Ruth declared.

Shortly after the family meeting, Hansel went to visit his father in jail. Vincent was relieved to see his son who has not visited him yet. They hugged each other and Hansel told his father that he was leaving the state to visit Jamaica. The name Jamaica set him up and he exclaimed, "Of all the islands, why Jamaica? What is there for you, son?" He replied to his father, "Of all the places on earth, why do you resent Jamaica, Dad?" And his father began to speak, "My mother has an archenemy still living in Kingston, Jamaica. Her name is Angelucia, a sorcerer who took away all of our inheritance because she loved my father, but he married my mother. She was barren and my mother had two boys to carry the Manchester last name. My brother and I are the only survivors of my father. He spent most of his life in Jamaica. He built an empire I was told, but Angelucia acquired this empire by magical spells. She is or was a sorcerer. She told my mother that she will turn us into drug addicts, thugs, if my mother did not agree to give up all the wealth in Jamaica, making her the only heiress of my dad. We only have what he had in the bank, cash insurance money and annuities. So, that is why I fear for you to go there. You can be killed. They are wild black folks who hate whites, especially that you are a Manchester."

Hansel said, "Rectification, Dad. You and I, we both know that blacks do not hate white. If they do, their reasons are based on history, not on color or race. The blacks do not care about our physical appearances. It is us who judge them by their appearance and their social-economic status. I am going to Jamaica. It is already planned. The story grandma told you is so inaccurate. In all respects, it is a pack of lies. If you knew the truth, you would be a different man today. You have a grudge implanted in you against blacks because of what your mother told you about one black person. I am normally a racist because I am white. Society bestowed that title on me. I must play by the rule. Nobody is born racist. Place a multicultural group of children together in a park to play. You will see they will play with each other without any discrimination. They do not understand the difference between them. However, as they grow older, they will drink the poison offered by society (racism) and they will learn to distance themselves from other people who are somehow different."

Vincent then inquired, "Hans, are you here to console me or to lecture me? I am paying for my crime. What else do you want me to do? By the way, how is Sarah doing? What did she say about me? How is the baby? Will Sara ever forgive me?" Hans replied, "I don't know, Dad. I have not spoken to her. You have a lot of damage control to do." Vincent kept on asking, "Will Sara come to visit me someday soon?" "Dad, I have no clue of what Sara is up to. I really do not. Do you know what the DNA test reveals?" He quickly replied, "I don't believe in those lab tests." "That you have a black ancestor from Madagascar. Your ancestors are all over the place. How do you feel about that, Dad?" He ignored him and Hans reminded him that being a racist is not positive. "You cannot let people know that you are racist. Why did you praise Adolf Hitler when talking to mom who is half Jewish and her grandparents died in the holocaust? Calling Hitler a great leader is outrageous and downright insensitive. He was a monster, a son of a . . . You must keep your racism for yourself like a lot of politicians do when they apply for office. They pretend to support blacks just to gain their vote. You understand what I mean? You cannot rub it in like that, Dad," Hans told his father. Vincent sighed and asked, "Would you talk to Sara on my behalf, son?" Hans replied, "If I were you, I would start by writing an apology letter to Will and his family. That is the only way to go; you sent him to prison. You must apologize even though the police will be sued for collaborating with you. They needed no evidence bringing him down. They did not investigate because he is black. It had to be him committing crime in the neighborhood where he was not welcome in the first place. You even made me believe that too, Dad. Well, I will see you when I get back from Jamaica." Vince hugged his son, sat down for a moment, held his head between his hands, thinking, "What am I going to tell Will?"

Two days later, his daughter Jennie came to visit him, the visit that will drag him into deep reflection. The eldest daughter told him the truth about Angelucia and the fortune in Jamaica that could have been his. He crumbled when he learned that the Mahoney brothers, Daniel and Dylan, are his half-siblings, two men of color that he came to admire because they are known for being shrewd businessmen. He held a bottle of their rum in his hands every holiday. He used to look at their pictures on the rum bottle and say, "Mahoney's Best rum." Jennie did not spare him. She told the truth just like it is.

Her grandmother is responsible for her father not inheriting his father's estate in Jamaica. Martha exchanged the name for the fortune just to keep the half-brothers and her sons apart, and that was a terrible shock to Vincent. And as much as he wanted to confront his eighty-two-year-old mother, he could not, because she was fighting dementia related to Alzheimer's disease. Soon after Jennie left, Ruth came to visit and told him that she is going to Jamaica on a cruise. "Are you going with Hans?" he asked. Ruth said, "No, he has not told me yet that he is leaving the state. I am going alone. I have a lot of thinking to do." Ruth did not mention anything about the family meeting and what was discussed. She was less chatty than usual.

Vince felt something. He wondered why Ruth does not speak much, so he asked her, "Ruthe, why are you so quiet? No more sermon for me?" She replied oddly, "Your mother had done enough preaching and she surely did a good job. I don't have to teach you anything anymore, Vince." This cold response troubled him. He kept silent until Ruth decided to leave. She gave him a hug and left quietly.

A week later, Vince was visited by his lawyer who was the good news bearer. Will and Sara made a plea to drop the charges against him. He was relieved and elated, and at the same time, ashamed. Will should hate him, but it was Will who encouraged Sara to drop the charge against her father. And William's parents who were devout Christians decided to accord clemency to the man who falsely accused their son.

Upon his return home, his wife was absent. She went on a cruise. His son was out of the state. Sara and the baby had gone to Africa with a Christian mission. Only Jennie was home to greet him. The white poodle puppy and the black kitty who are different species but have been getting along fine through the years were there to welcome him back home. Vincent left home to prison knowing that he was a pure white man. He came back with another sense of himself. Ethnically speaking, Vincent Manchester is a little bit of everything.

He felt happy to be free, but sad because all have changed. Nothing will be the same again in his household. Sara is no longer there. She went away with a baby in her arms, alone. He was wondering how Sara is going to manage in a mission, going around the world with a baby—a baby he wanted so much to meet and a daughter he missed so terribly. He dreamed of holding his first grandchild, but he missed that opportunity.

A few days after his release, he went to his desk and sat down to write the ultimate letter: "Dear Will, How did you find in your heart to forgive me, for what I did? I clearly do not deserve your clemency. I do not know how to express my gratitude to you, for giving me back my freedom. Undoubtedly, it is you who encouraged my daughter to drop the charges against me; therefore, making her forgive me too. Your action gave me back my faith in God. Goodness, kindness, compassion remind me there is God. I am an awful sinner, a haughty one. You forgive me, I thank you. I know you will never be thinking of me as a friend, but if you ever needed me, or my service, I will be there for you and will stand by you, young man. Likewise, if I ever need you, I will come to you. If a drop of my blood can save you, I will give it to you. If a drop of yours can save, you will save me. I respect you, for you have shown to be a better man than I could ever be, a man who is not all wrapped up in the superficialities of life. Today, I can take the liberty to quote, 'Once I was blind but now, I can see.'" After writing the letter, he asked himself, "What am I supposed to do with Rick? He raped my daughter. That is unacceptable and unforgettable, but forgivable, I suppose. If Will forgave me, forcibly, I must forgive Rick, but it is damn hard to do. I must forgive Rick, but I need time. How did Will forgive me? Does he really?"

When his wife came back from her trip, she brought him a bottle of Mahoney's best rum as a souvenir. She told him nothing about her visit in Jamaica. Vince looked at the bottle and saw the two faces of Dylan and Daniel Mahoney and he had a brilliant idea. He went to see Will Saint John with the rum bottle and made a request, "How would you feel if I commission you to make a portrait of those two men and insert my portrait in front of them or in the middle since I am younger?" Will smiled, scratching his head, and said, "Who are those men? Do you know them, Mr. Manchester? I do not want to be in trouble. Why do you want to reproduce their photography with you inserted in?" Vince replied, "They are my half-brothers from Jamaica." Will laughed and asked, "Are you serious, Mr. Manchester?" He spoke, "Profoundly serious. I chose you because you are a true artist, one with a soft touch. When it is done, write 'The Manchester Brothers.' By the way, have you heard anything from your friend Sara?" Will said, "No, I have not, but my girlfriend Lydia had. Sara is doing alright. Do not worry, Mr. Manchester, your daughter will come around. Family always comes around. She is your daughter." "Did she say anything about me at all to Leslie?" he continued asking. Will replied gently, "She asked Leslie if you were out of prison and how you look. That is all I know and as I told you, she will come around. Just give her time, you know." Vince was relieved and said, "Thank you, thank you, Will."

Effectively, when Will had finished the portrait, with Vince's portrait inserted in, he turned it into a large poster with the title "The Manchester Brothers." Upon completion of that project, Vince was fully satisfied with Will's work, and Will got paid generously for it.

Then, Vince sent the poster to Jamaica addressed to his half-brothers. Upon reception of such an unexpected gift from an estranged brother, Daniel and Dylan were elated. They said to each other, "Is he not he, little Vince, the one that came with our father when he was six years old?" They remembered that their father Samuel Manchester brought Vince to Jamaica when he was only six. Vince remembered vaguely the trip to Jamaica, but not the brothers who were also young at the time.

Infatuated by Vince's gesture, the two brothers who were overjoyed came to visit him, bringing him all kinds of goods from Jamaica, especially products from their industries. Vincent and his family received them with honor. It was a memorable brotherly reunion, a very emotional moment for the brothers who have been kept apart all those years by racism. Jason Manchester, the youngest brother, came with his family to meet his half-siblings that he never knew existed. He then apologized to them and praised them for keeping their father's legacy alive and therefore, making them all proud to be Manchester men. The news was all over in Jamaica. The newspapers reported that the two tycoons in Jamaica, Daniel and Dylan Mahoney, are really Manchester men.

Finally, Ruth and her husband came to terms in the matter of race. She was amazed by her husband's gesture of acknowledgment of his half-siblings. It was clear now that Vince was aware that racism is wrong and willing to change.

CHAPTER 14

Brooklyn County Jail

Eli and some other detainees are released. It is May. Wedding day at Capernaum is a big event. Eli must go. One of his mates asked him what changed his life from being an alcoholic, a lady's man, to a preacher. He replied, "All started in Capernaum. After my wife passed, I was depressed, lonely. I was looking for some comfort, so I went to visit a young woman who was also looking for comfort and intimacy. We got together and we were in bed making out when all of sudden, cars were beeping, there were a lot of commotions in the streets, and somebody yelled, 'Jesus is in town, come out all you, bring your burden, the last night rain has healing power, the Lord is in town, come out you all!'

The woman I was with got up, put a scarf over her head, and ran out, forgetting me laying down in her bed. I said, 'Do not leave me like that. Where are my pants?' She said, 'The Lord is in town and you are talking about your pants. I want to be saved, I do not need you, you are fornicating. I am out of here. Jesus is in town. Oh my God!" The inmates asked, "What do they mean by Jesus is in town?"

Eli said, "Let me explain. There was a young girl in town named Sadia. She was homeless. Her mother died leaving her with her siblings. Because Sadia was disfigured badly, her face was always covered. Because she was hideous and presumed to be contagious, no one has ever seen her face. The siblings had left town leaving her behind. The pastors provided food and clothes for her in the street. She spent her time mostly at the city gate. She was religious, always singing for people who would give her money and clothes. Her family was originally from Ethiopia. She was a Jewish girl who was converted to Christianity by the pastors who were helping her out. She learned to read and write in the street. Every Friday around six in the evening, one could hear her singing a Hebrew song that nobody understood. Shema Israel! Shema Ethiopia! Adonai Elohim, Adonai Echad . . . She observed the Sabbath even though she was Christian. She referred to herself as Messianic Jewish. She would go around greeting people Shabbat Shalom on Saturdays and still will attend Sunday service, outside the church of course. Because her disease was supposedly contagious, she could not get in.

Two days preceding the collective wedding days at Capernaum, it rained a different kind of rain. The streets were waterlogged. The rainwater was warm and smelled like sulfur. People were questioning why the rainwater was so warm and had a smell.

Sadia reported that she was praying to God to change her face to make her an acceptable human being. During the rain, as she laid down, she heard a voice that said, 'Get up, Sadia, get up, remove your veil, go to the rain, remain there till the rain stops, and go to sleep. Tomorrow will be a brighter day for you. You will show the world your face.' She said smiling, 'Who are you! You are pulling a prank on me. It's not April first. No April fool?' The voice replied, 'Sadia, this is Jesus your Lord. Just do as I tell you to.' She exclaimed, 'Jesus! The Lord! Is it a prank?' It was too good to be true for her. She still did not believe it was a divine command she received, but she went out in the rain and remained till the rain subsided. Then, she went to bed in her wet clothes. In the morning, her face was cleared of the awful skin disease that had plagued her since childhood sloughed off. It was not leper but a severe case of psoriasis. When she got up from her bed, all the sloughed skin was laid on her couch. She looked at them with disgust. Then, she ran to her pastor to tell of the miracle and it was the pastor who communicated the news to the media.

A beautiful rainbow appeared in the sky. Jesus was in town and people really believed that Jesus was in town, and they came out singing glorious songs, walking around the city with palm branches in their hands. The anterior of all houses was embellished with decorative ornaments. Those who had enemies went on to ask for forgiveness and offered peace. A man went to another man to pay his long due debt. Some were looking for a drop of the rainwater to put in a bottle to become a relic.

It was reported that the rainwater cured a blind man who washed his face with it. The pastor so excited and spiritually empowered screamed from the top of his lungs saying, 'O Capernaum, small city of US, you are not the least of all the cities for today, you have seen the might and the glory of God. Jesus has visited us in Capernaum. How awesome!'

Sadia was placed on top of a car. Everybody could see that the girl who was once rejected, now was a celebrity in the same town that rejected her. Her skin looked smooth and immaculate. Her hair was beautiful. Everyone, even me, had a song to sing. On that day, I also found salvation. I followed the preacher to the spring and got baptized.

In the evening, there was an assembly at the city gate. A Jewish girl sang one of the most moving Hebrew songs— Avinu Malkeinu (Our Father, Our King) in Hebrew. And surprisingly, Sadia joined her in the English version of that song. The crowd was so moved by the songs that many accepted Yeshua as their savior and the way to God. From that time on, every time it rains, people came out to be wet by the rainwater, hoping to be healed physically, emotionally, and spiritually.

"What happened to Sadia after that?" asked a listener.

Eli replied, "She remained in Capernaum and became an evangelist and the leader of the Christian ministry there. People flocked to Capernaum just to meet her and hear her experience with God. Consequently, people who believed accepted the word of God. The next day was the collective wedding in Capernaum. The city was ready to celebrate. Everyone who wanted to be married could get married free of charge. The mayor, the parish, and the evangelical community arranged for the wedding to be a special event. Visitors, guests, all were welcome to Capernaum for the big event that takes place every five years. Unfortunately, for two men who came to get married, they were turned down.

At the city gate, the clerk told them that same-sex marriage is not allowed in Capernaum. One of the men said, 'This is United States.' The clerk responded ironically, 'This is Capernaum. It is not a state and it is not united. I am sorry. But you are welcome to celebrate with the others. We love you, brothers, but we just cannot marry you. There is nothing wrong with two men loving each other, but sex cannot be involved. Love is not the problem here. It is sex. You cannot and should not have sex with each other, period.' They replied, 'Listen, Mr. We came here to get married, not to be moralized. You sound so self-righteous.' The clerk replied, 'Well, I don't make the law. You can go somewhere else and get hitched.' 'We will do so. You are such a clown,' they said as they were leaving. They went to the wedding ceremony and party afterward." "What happened to your girlfriend?" an inmate asked. Eli answered, "I met her at the river. She accepted the Lord and got baptized. A woman called Delia who owned a brothel closed her door forever. Surprisingly, on the wedding day, one of her clients, a man who likes her, had made arrangements to marry her. Delia cried with joy, 'Thank you, God! Thank you. A man has finally made a respectable woman of me. He really loves me enough to marry me, not for sex but for me. Thank God.'"

"Did you get married after that, Eli?" one person asked. He answered, "Yes, I did, and this time, I was a better husband, but my wife died, and that was the second woman. I realize that I am the angel of death. So, I remain celibate. I read the bible, teach Sunday school, and preach in the street to keep myself in line. I am afraid of getting married again." "Well, you do not have to get married to enjoy life, Eli. Have a steady girlfriend," an inmate commented. "No, I cannot. It is not acceptable by the church. If I am preaching, I cannot be living in sins," Eli explained. The other man replied, "That is bullshit. If you have a steady girlfriend, it is not a sin. You sin when you are going around having sex with different mates. You are living your life according to the church. Where in the bible did Noah get married, and by whom?" Eli, very unsure of what to say, stuttered, "I, I, truly do not know, but the fact remains. I cannot be a teacher of the bible while I am not committed to a woman. That is just the way it is, I cannot. Besides, I am getting old, you know. Sex is not like it used to be when I was young. Now, I am just looking for a companion, someone to talk to." "You are looking for intimacy, Eli, we all do. Even when we are old, intimacy is still part of life. You would like someone to touch you, to blow softly into your ears, caress you tenderly. It is much better than when you are doing it to yourself, man. You miss that, man, come on. Do not go around the bushes denying it. Say it, you miss intimacy. It does not help to deny your feeling. God gave us all those emotions. Those emotions bring out feelings. That is all."

Eli said, "Well, I hear you, I hear you. You are right. To sum up, guys, it was a pleasure to meet you all. I will miss you. As you can see, our storytelling started with the devil coming to town and finished with Jesus coming to town. Do you all see the difference between the arrival of the devil and the arrival of Jesus? Capernaum had changed forever. Today, it's the center of gospel ministry, just like it was in biblical time, the center of Jesus' ministry. Since then, Capernaum is known as one the safest cities in the US—lowest in crimes, clear of drugs, economically flourishing. So, I am going back to Capernaum, the Lord's favorite city."

Eli left the prison. He went home to visit his family and especially his daughter Simone who was supposed to be married to Walter at the Capernaum weddings. But unfortunately, Simone has postponed her wedding because she is tested positive for coronavirus. Walt was distressed and disappointed. He will not be going to Capernaum to watch Emilie getting married but will remain in town to support his ailing fiancée. Emilie and her fiancé will travel to Capernaum to get married. Her sister Kate and her son Kendall will be there to support her.

The mayor, pastors, and priest reminded people of the impending danger of the coronavirus. The wedding at Capernaum is not the same this year because of the pandemic. Social distancing does not allow a large crowd. During the marriage ceremony, a moment of silence was observed for those who had to postpone due to illness. Among the names cited were the names of Simone Davenport and Walter Johnson who could not be there because of Corona. Emilie said, "Simone Davenport and Walter Johnson, do I hear it correctly?"

Kendall said, "Walter Johnson, that is right, my father, and that woman Simone Davenport." Emilie said, "I know Simone. She has a son called Benjamin surnamed Benji. It has to be the same Simone. I met her in jail." Kendall said, "I know Benji Davenport. He is my tennis partner." Emilie trembled and spoke, "Maybe your brother too. Is it possible that Simone is Walter's girlfriend in high school that got pregnant? My Lord! All are making sense now. This is the same Simone. Mine, oh mine! What a small world! You and Benji are brothers." Kendall smiled and spoke, "What are you talking about, Mom? How can suddenly Benji go from being my tennis partner to my half-brother? How do you know that?" "Let us observe that moment of silence and pray for them. I will explain all to you later. That goddamned coronavirus is getting under people's skin. How come a simple virus can make the world stand still?" asked Emilie.

Errol Francis is released. Before going to the twelve steps program for alcoholism, he wanted to visit Capernaum. Before leaving New York, Eli went to see his daughter Simone who was COVID-19 positive. Grace is very depressed, and Eli felt his daughter's anguish and there was nothing he could do to help her. He decided to fast and pray for a miracle. He remembered Sadia the girl that everybody despised because of her bizarre appearance and remembered that God listened to her prayer and healed her. Eli is going to Capernaum not for the wedding festivities but for a miracle. Erroll Francis is tagging along. Both men were on a mission. Erroll is looking for sobriety and Eli is supplicating for his daughter and granddaughter in troubles. They arrived in Capernaum two days before the wedding. The city was beautiful. A sense of spirituality was in the air. At the entrance, a big poster was advertised for God. It reads: God exists, he is everywhere, but if you make a special place in your heart for him, he will come and reside forever. The other ad reads: Jesus is real. He lives in Capernaum. He is the guest of honor to our weddings. The church bells were playing the most beautiful and joyful hymns that rejoiced the hearts of all visitors and pilgrims.

Eli and Errol went to a river nearby where people were getting immersed for baptism. There, the two men remained all day in a fasting state. At evenfall, they were hungry. They stopped by a restaurant for a meal before going home. Errol was going to stay with

Eli for a couple of days. As soon as they started eating their meal, the evening news came on, and the headline said: An unidentified paralyzed young woman who has not spoken for years gave birth at seven months. The baby weighs six pounds and in stable condition. The mother who has not communicated for years spoke and is concerned about her twins she had sixteen years ago.

At the same moment, Eli's phone rang. It is Grace calling her father with the news. It is Lauralee who gave birth unexpectedly at seven months instead of nine. Most importantly, she can speak and remember her twins. She said she has identical twins. Grace is in shock and amazed that her daughter can now speak and remember certain things.

Eli and Errol left their foods, paid, tipped, and then went out, dancing to the sound of "Glory Be to God." The two men danced and attracted a crowd who started singing and dancing with them. Eli explained to the crowd that they came for a miracle and they got a miracle. Furthermore, he explained that the unidentified paralyzed woman who gave birth in the news is Lauralee, his granddaughter who is back to life, and it is a big relief for his daughter Grace.

According to Grace, Lauralee gave birth but does not bond with the newborn. Instead, she kept asking who that baby is and where the father is. Then, she asked for her twins. When they came to see her, she claimed to have had identical girls, and how come those two girls do not look identical? To that question, Grace was speechless, and the girls were rather sad. Their mother rejected them. Grace tried to make them understand that their mother is not one hundred percent herself yet and that in time, she will love them. But at the same time, she was thinking about Melony's girls. They are identical, Deborah and Anna, so much so that Grace does not even know which one is which. Eli then inquired about Lauralee's mobility, "Can she walk now?" Grace replied, "Lauralee insisted on getting out of bed by herself soon after giving birth. She tried. She almost fell, but the physical therapist said she will walk again even though he cannot explain how the birth brings so many changes in her condition. And as of now, Lauralee is no longer classified as paraplegic. Her muscles are weak now because she has been bedridden for so long. But since she is mentally capable and willing to walk again, she will eventually do. She simply needs time to strengthen her muscles. I am so thankful. I don't even know how to express my gratitude to God." She wept.

CHAPTER 15

After the festivities at Capernaum, the two men returned to New York to visit Lauralee and be partakers of a big Thanksgiving celebration for Lauralee's return to normal life. But there was one setback—the newborn was taken by social services until further action. First, because Lauralee was not fit yet to be a mother. There was no bonding between her and the baby. Second, she was living in the past, asking for her twin babies she had sixteen years ago. Thirdly, she seemed angry, refusing to hold the infant, insisting that she sees the father. Finally, she claimed that she does not like boys. She wants her identical twin girls. The rehab facility called Children Services to intervene to protect the infant boy. So, he was taken into foster care temporarily until his mother or an eligible relative can be granted custody for kinship.

* * *

Philadelphia State Penitentiary

It is December 18, 2018. Urma Thompson, thirty-seven years old, has been arrested for stolen identity—social security fraud. She is highly anxious and alone. Her living boyfriend had just deployed to Iraq. A week later, she requested to see a Catholic chaplain. Her request was granted. Father Mclowski was assigned to her as counselor and chaplain. So, he came to see her. They greet each other cordially and then Urma said, "Do you know why I am here, Father?" He answered no and added, "I am here to hear, to listen not to question, nor to judge you. Now, how can I help you?" Urma replied, "I have been living as a fugitive for years." The priest was surprised and exclaimed, "Fugitive! May I ask why you are a fugitive?" Urma responded, "It's a long story. You need to sit down to hear me out. I was wanted by the police to question the accidental death of my stepfather. I had a baby at 17. My stepfather arranged for the baby to be taken away from me. Children Services came to the hospital and took the baby. It was a boy. I named him Dodie. He was so cute. I loved my baby so much I would do anything to raise him. My stepfather was a tyrant because he was always right and must have the last word. When I became pregnant, he told me that I must go away. My siblings should not know that I am pregnant because that would set a bad example. He declared he would not accept any pregnancy unless the other party wants to get married. At sixteen, he wanted me to marry the father of my unborn baby or go live with his family. I did not know the family. They did not know me. Robert and I were both teenagers who have nothing but schoolbooks." Mclowski said, "Was he really a tyrant or simply an old-fashioned man who believed in marriage as the foundation of a family?" Peggy said, "Well, we were kids." Mclowski said, "And kids should not engage in sexual activities. You should have thought of that, don't you think?" She continued, "Anyway, he was the breadwinner in the family. Therefore, my mother had no say in anything. She approved of everything he said. I was sent away to live in a home for unwed mothers. When I was due to deliver the baby, I returned to Troy, my hometown. I could stay in the hospital before delivery. I had a healthy baby boy that I named Dodie. I was so happy to see my son. He was somehow special. He had twelve little fingers and twelve little toes, a genetic anomaly that runs in my boyfriend's family.

When it was time to go home, I was told that social service has the baby. He will not be delivered to me. His placement was pre-arranged. I asked, who has him? Where did he go? The nurse could not tell. She did not know. And everything was confidential. So, I left the hospital empty-handed. You can imagine my pain and my sorrow after nine months of discomfort, nine months away from home, no family around, and nine months of loneliness except the expectation of a child. Then, I left the hospital without my Dodie. I never knew what happened to Dodie.

Shortly after that, my mother encouraged me to enroll in high school. I did, and I graduated. As for my boyfriend, I have not seen him. His parents had moved away. So, I was alone and empty. I resented my stepfather. He was my father's brother. After dad died, he lost his wife and had three adolescent sons and a little girl Alma who needed a mother. So, my uncle then chose my mom to be his spouse. She asked us if we will be comfortable with our uncle marrying her. We said yes because we needed a father figure at the time and he was well off. He was also pleasant then; also very generous with us. Big mistake mom made. He was a dictator, an authoritarian. He made our lives a living hell. Everything was no. The house had to be spotless every day all the time. We were always reading something. He would question about the book we read at dinner time. There were bible verses to memorize and school assignments to be checked every night. He was never tired. He said we have to strive for perfection in life. He showed no affection to any one of us, even for one of his sons, Lucas, who was mentally challenged." The priest said, "He was very stern." "Yes, he was as opposed to my father," Urma said. "I hated him for taking my son away from me. I wished him to die of natural death, so we all could be free, but I never thought of murdering him. Unfortunately, the worst happened when I was twenty years old. My stepfather fell off the balcony and died instantly. Although I did not like him, I mourned him. I felt sad and even guilty for not liking him and when I look back, he was not that bad. I would never want such a gruesome death for him. His mentally unstable son told the police that I made his father fall. The police believed him and was after me for questioning. My siblings encouraged me to leave town. So, I left without even saying goodbye to my mother. My youngest sister, Danielle, begged me to write to her, but I did not. I was afraid. I was so certain the police were after me. I made the mistake of not reporting for the interrogation. I did not know what the outcome will be.

As I was leaving, I took my dead sister Urma Thompson's birth certificate and social security. I went to New York first, then I came to Philadelphia and became Urma Thompson. My real name is Peggy Armstrong. My eldest sister Urma was from my mother's first husband, Gregory Thompson, who divorced shortly after Urma's birth.

I requested to see you for another issue, my conscience. Last year, I wanted to see my mother so much and see my hometown, my home. I was dying of nostalgia. I decided to drive to Troy, intending to simply take a glimpse at my neighborhood, hoping to see my mother or one of my siblings from afar.

When I got there, nothing was the same. Everything has changed—the house was empty, my next-door neighbor's house was burned down, my street was desolate, and a few houses were boarded down. I did not see anyone that I knew. I drove to a nearby mall hoping to see my mother taking a stroll to the mall or to the store. I missed her so much. I keep remembering her favorite song, "I Did It My Way." She would hum that tune all the time. I stopped by a donut shop drive-thru to get something to eat. Suddenly, I saw the cops. I got panicked I backed up and turned around to avoid the police. I got away, but I hit someone. I saw the woman on the ground, but I had no courage to stop because I was afraid of the police. I fled from the scene. I felt bad, guilty. I was on edge praying that the person is not dead. I went to my hotel to pack. It was about 5 PM. I turned the TV on. I got the worst news of my entire life. The hit and run, who the woman was, Father, can you guess who I hit and run from?" The priest said, "No, I cannot guess. Who was she?" Urma replied, "My mother, I had the chance to see the face of my siblings on Television begging the person who did it to come forward. I cried like I never did in my whole life. Fortunately, the news mentioned that she was in stable condition. She suffered from broken hips and broken legs. She could be paralyzed. Nobody knows about that. You are the first person I confide to. I will tell all to the court to free my conscience."

"How about the identity theft? Why now did the police come after you? What brings that up?" She answered, "I wanted to surprise my boyfriend when he gets back from the service with a new house we have been renting. I applied for the loan. I was waiting for an answer from the bank. Instead, it was the police who came to question me about my identity. They said that according to the record, Urma Thompson died many years ago. I did not deny it. I told the truth which is I am Peggy Armstrong, the second child of Wilbur and Amelia Armstrong. Urma Thompson was my half-sister. She died five years ago. They said, 'You have to come with us. You are under arrest for identity theft.' I said, 'Yes, officer.' I offered my hands. I went with them without any fuss, any murmur. I deserve to be in jail. However, I did not orchestrate my stepfather's death. Father, do you think I was destined to go to prison? Do you believe in destiny?" The priest replied, "I am not sure about destiny. Do you realize that you just confessed a crime to me? I suppose to keep it for myself. How do you want me to help you? I cannot condemn or forgive people. I am a sinner myself with my bag of sins. What do you expect from me? Tell me, how I can help you? Only God forgives and condemns." Peggy declared, "My only wish is to see my son one day. I would like to know where Dodie is. He must be eighteen years old now and there is something distinct about him." "What is that?" Father Mclowski asked. Peggy said, "He has twelve fingers and twelve toes." Mclowski asked, "Where was he born? Where are you from exactly?" "I am from the city of Troy in Oakland County, Michigan," Peggy answered. Father Maclowski asked, "What was the baby's full name at birth?" She replied, "I named him Dodie, Alexander Ramos." Mclowski inquired, "Is Ramos the father's family name?" Peggy nodded yes and broke into tears asking, "Will I be found guilty, Father?"

"Before entering priesthood, I was an attorney ad litem," Father declared and Peggy asked, "What does that mean, ad litem?" Mclowski explained, "It is a lawyer appointed by the court to represent children or minors and advocate for their interests. I no longer practice law. I am a clergyman. However, I can try to see what I can come up with. As for the case of being accused of sabotage in your stepfather's accidental death, I have one question for you. Why did you skip town instead of talking to the police since you were innocent you did not do anything wrong? Tell me, what went through your mind that had made you run away and even change your name and never contact your parents for all those years?" Peggy still in tears replied, "I was only twenty. I did not know any better. I was scared. I have heard of innocent people who spent years behind bars, Father."

"Did your boyfriend know all about your past including your fake identity?" She said, "No, I never told him the truth about me. I let him know that my parents were both dead. He knows about my son being in a foster home. I did not trust him enough to tell him that the police were looking for me. Father, I really messed up my life. I do not feel terrible for using my sister's identity. I feel bad for the hit and run. That is what is eating me. The fault nobody knows about is the one nagging me, Father. I am somehow relieved today that I finally clear my conscience, at last. I talk to someone about it. I tell the truth. Is there any redemption for me, Father, is there? I am willing to be punished for my unacceptable behavior, but I am not ready to hear a jury say, 'Accused, stand up, you are guilty.' I am afraid of facing a court, a judge, and a jury, and most of all, to hear a verdict."

Mcloswski said, "To be pardoned for everything, you must tell the whole truth and nothing but the truth, and God will set you free. One mistake brought on another. Taking your baby away from you without your consent, to never see him again, was not fair and that will melt a juror's heart. What was your boyfriend's name?" "Roberto Ramos," she replied. McClowski stated, "This is what I am going to do for you to relieve your high anxiety. I will contact the police in Troy about your stepfather's cold case. If there was ever a case, you probably made yourself a fugitive for no reason. Then, I will contact someone in Children Services to see about your son's whereabouts. Now, let us pray?" Peggy felt that a load is off her shoulder. Finally, help is on the way. They prayed and before the priest left, he said, "I forgot to ask you. What was your stepfather's name?" She replied, "Randall Armstrong and my father were Wilbur Armstrong. My mother is Amelia King." Mclowski asked, "When did your stepfather die?" Peggy responded, "On March 24, 2003. I was then 20 years old." "Where did you go before coming to Philadelphia?" asked the priest. Peggy said, "I went to New York." "Thank you. I will contact you as soon as I find out something vital to your case. May God be with you." Peggy said, "Thank you, Father, for listening to my troubles." "Jesus can redeem you. I guarantee you that," he said and left.

An inmate came and said to Peggy, "What took you so long? He has been talking to you for over an hour. What did you have to say to him? He is a sinner like you. Do not tell him everything. Do not spill the beans, girl. By the way, can we vote?" Peggy said, "I suppose we can. We are citizens of this country. Every single citizen has the constitutional right to vote, even the worst criminal." She sighed and said, "There was a time when women and blacks had no right to vote. Do you know that?" Peggy replied, "Oh yeah, I know, that is history. We have the privilege to vote now and we should vote." Then, the inmate presented herself as Martha Morrow and said to Peggy, "I am a democrat, but I have been hearing that nonsense on the television." "What nonsense?" Peggy inquired. Martha explained, "They are saying that the country is now divided. Why do they say that now? This country has always been divided from the start. There was always North and South who did not agree, so much so they faced up each other in a bloody civil war. Blacks and whites were, are, and will always be divided by bigotry. Politically speaking, Republicans and Democrats are always at each other's throats. In terms of religion, Christians, Jews, and Muslims despise each other. The poor and the rich still do not mingle. Lately, we have the police and the black community who do not get along. So, when was this country united?" Peggy said ironically, "Only the states are united to form this nation. That is all." Martha said, "You cannot trust anything they are saying. The country is now divided. That's bullshit."

Mclowski did investigate and found out that the Armstrong case was close because he fell as the result of a massive stroke and there was no evidence to support that Peggy set up the fall. He also learned that Dodie Ramos was in kinship care instead of foster care. According to the Children Services agency, when a woman named Nadia Jimenez and her husband Alonzo Jimenez applied for foster parent care, they were offered Dodie Ramos, and the social worker told them that the child is healthy except for one oddity. He has twelves fingers and toes. Nadia was in dismay because she is a Ramos and her brothers all have extra digits, a genetic anomaly in the Ramos family. She became curious and questioned the agency about Dodie's mother. The agency did not say much about her since she did not sign any paper placing the child in foster care prior to adoption. Nadia requested kinship care instead of foster care because she passionately believed she is related to the child. Nevertheless, Social Services denied the request, stating that was not enough to establish kinship and qualify her as a family member. The Jimenez did not argue. They accepted Dodie as a foster child. Soon after, they got custody of the infant. They did a DNA test that proved Dodie and Nadia are very close relatives. Consequently, they were approved for kinship care.

Two years later, Dodie was adopted by the Jimenezes. That was the best news Father Mclowski had to deliver to Peggy. Then, he got the word that Amelia, Peggy's mother, was living in a rehabilitation facility. As a priest, he could go visit. He visited her and she started telling him about her life. Amelia confessed to him that she is partly responsible for Peggy leaving town, "I did not support my daughter when I should. I had a doubt. Peggy resented my husband so much. For a moment, I thought, maybe she had something to do with the fall. I was simply filled with grief. Imagine, Father, I lost two husbands to death and one to divorce. It seems like my life is paved with misfortunes. My first husband was Gregory Thompson. We were married when we were only twenty-one, college freshmen who had nothing but our schoolbooks. I went to live with his family, and I was not happy at all." "Why was that?" asked the priest. Amelia said, "I felt that I was just another child. I was controlled, criticized, and even bullied." "How?" the priest inquired. "I was supposed to serve my husband, do his laundry, serve him his foods like his mother does for his father. They were from island and very old-fashioned. I watch my father-in-law slap Gregory once." "Slap, mm, that sounds a little extreme," the priest commented. Amelia explained, "Greg had changed his major from premed to sociology. His father was furious. He said to him that he expected him to be a physician because it is a noble occupation with high social status and most of all, an occupation that provides financial security. As a result of that, I decided to go back to my family. Gregory agreed to move with me, but when he told his parents, the father had a fit. He screamed, 'You are moving to the Jones. You are going to curl up in your wife's little bedroom and be a burden to the Jones. Over my dead body, no son of mine would do such a thing. You will lose your respect and will never get it back. Where is your pride, son?' Gregory responded, 'The bible says that a man should leave his family to be with his wife.' The father replied, 'Don't you dare lecture me, boy. How many men in the bible and today follow their wives? The bible also says: you shall not fornicate, which you did. You forgot this precept when you were unfastening your zipper.' Gregory listened to him. Eventually, I left their household without my husband. He came very often to see the baby and provide emotional support and as little financial aid as he could. Then, he decided to enroll in the air force. In his absence, I fell in love with Wilbur. I divorced him and that was the end. He went to Vietnam and came back a broken man."

The priest asked, "How so? He should come back as a hero." Amelia replied, "Quiet the contrary. He came back more like a zero. He suffered from post-traumatic stress syndrome and one day, he committed suicide." "I am so sorry, that is sad." And she added, "My daughter Urma died in a car crash and then my second husband died of a heart attack, my third of a massive stroke, and my daughter ran away never to come back. If she is alive, God protect her and if she is dead, may thy will be done. So, her soul is in your hands."

Amelia burst into tears. Mclowski simply reassured her that Peggy is not dead and then, when it's least expected, she will pop up. They prayed together and Amelia was content and hoping that Peggy will come back home someday soon. She said, "Father, what a relief it is to talk to someone who listens. I am hoping that Peggy is alive. You sound so positive like you know something I do not and that is enough consolation for my grieving soul."

A month later, Father Mclowski returned to the state penitentiary to visit Peggy to deliver the good news. Peggy was so happy that she cried with joy. She said she was no longer afraid to go to court and tell the story of her life. It all started when she met a boy in high school called Roberto Ramos. She fell in love. Her mother warned her about intimacy, but she would not listen. She got pregnant and her stepfather would not accept the pregnancy or the baby to be raised in the family with an unwed mother. He believed that would be a disgrace and would bring shame to his family.

Father Mclowski made sure that a good attorney is appointed to Peggy.

As advised by the priest, in the court, she told the whole truth and nothing but the truth. It was a short trial and after three days of deliberation, the jury had found Peggy Armstrong not guilty. Filled with joy, she hugged Father Mclowski to thank him and she said, "Father, tomorrow is a new day for me." Father said, "I know, I know, everything turns out in your favor, praise God for that. So, what is the plan now?" Peggy said, "I am going back to Troy to see my mother and my sisters and brothers wherever they are, and I will look for my son. I dream of Dodie every single day. Not a day has passed without thinking of him, my boy." Father said, "His adoptive name is Eduardo Ramos Jimenez. Remember that if you want to find him. Goodbye, Peggy." They hugged each other one more time for the last time.

Shortly after, Peggy was released from prison. The priest sent her a note telling her not to surprise her mother. After such a long absence, she must prepare her mother and other relatives for her coming back home. A surprise can be too much of an excitement for an aging heart. Peggy wrote to her mother and siblings announcing her arrival. Before she left the prison, she complained to her fellow prisoner about her financial situation. She has no money to pay an investigator to look for her son. Martha told her, "Do not worry about money. Freedom is better than money. Besides, who knows? Your son is probably looking for you." On the day before Thanksgiving, Peggy packed and left Philadelphia for Troy. She stopped to spend a night in a hotel. She got in the hotel elevator with a few people. She got off on the fourth floor and walked to her room 409. In room 411 is Roberto Ramos and his wife. They were altogether in the elevator. Roberto spotted her. At the desk, he left a note for her. To the hotel valet, he said, "Would you please give this note to the lady in room 409?" And the clerk said, "Miss Peggy Armstrong." Roberto said, "Yes." The note said, "Did you go to Holy Trinity High? You remind me of someone that was once close to me. I am Roberto Ramos, here is my cell number . . ."

Marie-Ghislaine Mera
6243 Carpenter street
Philadelphia
Pa 19143
Phone: 215-472-2370
Cell: 215 -839-4418
Email: marie.mera@outlook.com

www.ingramcontent.com/pod-product-compliance
Lightning Source LLC
Chambersburg PA
CBHW030637190726
48286CB00008B/2562